高一同學的目標

1. 熟背「高中常用7000字」

2. 月期考得高分

3. 會說流利的英語

1.「用會話背7000字①」書 + CD 280元

以三個極短句為一組的方式，讓同學背了會話，
同時快速增加單字。高一同學要從「國中常用
2000字」挑戰「高中常用7000字」，加強單字是
第一目標。

2.「一分鐘背9個單字」書 + CD 280元

利用字首、字尾的排列，讓你快速增 ⋯
一個字簡單。

3. rival

rival⁵ ('raɪvl̩) n. 對手
arrival³ (ə'raɪvl̩) n. 到達   } 都有 rival
festival² ('fɛstəvl̩) n. 節日；慶祝活動

revival⁶ (rɪ'vaɪvl̩) n. 復甦
survival³ (sə'vaɪvl̩) n. 生還   } 字尾是 vival
carnival⁶ ('karnəvl̩) n. 嘉年華會

carnation⁵ (kar'neʃən) n. 康乃馨
donation⁶ (do'neʃən) n. 捐贈   } 字尾是 nation
donate⁶ ('donet) v. 捐贈

3.「一口氣考試英語」書 + CD 280元

把大學入學考試題目編成會話，背了以後，
會說英語，又會考試。

例如：
> What a nice surprise! (真令人驚喜！)【常考】
> I can't believe my eyes.
> (我無法相信我的眼睛。)
> *Little did I dream of seeing you here.*
> (做夢也沒想到會在這裡看到你。)【駒澤大】

4.「一口氣背文法」書＋CD 280元
英文文法範圍無限大，規則無限多，誰背得完？
劉毅老師把文法整體的概念，編成216句，背完
了會做文法題、會說英語，也會寫作文。既是一
本文法書，也是一本會話書。

1. 現在簡單式的用法

I *get up* early every day.	我每天早起。
I *understand* this rule now.	我現在了解這條規定了。
Actions *speak* louder than words.	行動勝於言辭。

【二、三句強調實踐早起】

5.「高中英語聽力測驗①」書＋MP3 280元
6.「高中英語聽力測驗進階」書＋MP3 280元
高一月期考聽力佔20%，我們根據大考中心公布的
聽力題型編輯而成。

7.「高一月期考英文試題」書＋CD 280元
收集建中、北一女、師大附中、中山、成功、景
美女中等各校試題，並聘請各校名師編寫模擬試
題。

8.「高一英文克漏字測驗」書 180元
9.「高一英文閱讀測驗」書 180元
全部取材自高一月期考試題，英雄
所見略同，重複出現的機率很高。
附有翻譯及詳解，不必查字典，對
錯答案都有明確交待，做完題目，
一看就懂。

高二同學的目標──提早準備考大學

1.「用會話背7000字①②」
書+CD，每冊280元

「用會話背7000字」能夠解決
所有學英文的困難。高二同學
可先從第一冊開始背，第一冊
和第二冊沒有程度上的差異，
背得越多，單字量越多，在腦
海中的短句越多。每一個極短句大多不超過5個字，1個字或
2個字都可以成一個句子，如：「用會話背7000字①」p.184，
每一句都2個字，好背得不得了，而且與生活息息相關，是
每個人都必須知道的知識，例如：成功的祕訣是什麼？

11. What are the keys to success?

Be *ambitious*.	要有**雄心**。
Be *confident*.	要有**信心**。
Have *determination*.	要有**決心**。
Be *patient*.	要有**耐心**。
Be *persistent*.	要有**恆心**。
Show *sincerity*.	要有**誠心**。
Be *charitable*.	要有**愛心**。
Be *modest*.	要**虛心**。
Have *devotion*.	要**專心**。

當你背單字的時候，就要有「雄心」，要「決心」背好，對
自己要有「信心」，一定要有「耐心」和「恆心」，背書時
要「專心」。

背完後，腦中有2,160個句子，那不得了，無限多的排列組
合，可以寫作文，有了單字，翻譯、閱讀測驗、克漏字都難
不倒你了。高二的時候，要下定決心，把7000字背熟、背
爛。雖然高中課本以7000字為範圍，編者為了便宜行事，
往往超出7000字，同學背了少用的單字，反倒忽略真正重要
的單字。千萬記住，背就要背「高中常用7000字」，背完之
後，天不怕、地不怕，任何考試都難不倒你。

2.「時速破百單字快速記憶」書 + CD 280元

字尾是 try，重音在倒數第三音節上

entry³ ('ɛntrɪ) n. 進入【No entry. 禁止進入。】
country¹ ('kʌntrɪ) n. 國家；鄉下【ou 讀 /ʌ/，為例外字】
ministry⁴ ('mɪnɪstrɪ) n. 部【mini = small】

chemistry⁴ ('kɛmɪstrɪ) n. 化學
geometry⁵ (dʒɪ'ɑmətrɪ) n. 幾何學【geo 土地, metry 測量】
industry² ('ɪndəstrɪ) n. 工業；勤勉【這個字重音常唸錯】

poetry¹ ('po‧ɪtrɪ) n. 詩
poultry⁴ ('poltrɪ) n. 家禽 ⎱字尾 y 表「集合名詞」
pastry⁵ ('pestrɪ) n. 糕餅 ⎰

3.「高二英文克漏字測驗」書 180元

4.「高二英文閱讀測驗」書 180元
全部選自各校高二月期考試題精華，英雄所見略同，再出現的機率很高。

5.「7000字學測英文模擬試題詳解」書280元
一般模考題為了便宜行事，往往超出7000字範圍，無論做多少份試題，仍然有大量生字，無法進步。唯有鎖定7000字為範圍的試題，才會對準備考試有幫助。每份試題都經「劉毅英文」同學實際考過，效果奇佳。附有詳細解答，單字標明級數，對錯答案都有明確交待，不需要再查字典，做完題目，再看詳解，快樂無比。

6.「高中常用7000字解析【豪華版】」書 390元
按照「大考中心高中英文參考詞彙表」編輯而成。難背的單字有「記憶技巧」、「同義字」及「反義字」，關鍵的單字有「典型考題」。大學入學考試核心單字，以紅色標記。

7.「高中7000字測驗題庫」書 180元
取材自大規模考試，解答詳盡，節省查字典的時間。

寫英文作文很簡單

　　之前出了一本「一口氣背同義字寫作文…①」，原理是外國人寫文章時，避免重複，往往會用同義字取代。如目標是 goal，就背 goal-target-purpose，aim-plan-objective，對寫作文有很大的幫助。如 You must have a *goal*. You must have a *purpose*. The most important part of success is choosing an *objective*. 加上轉承語，就快速寫出文章。

　　美國人不論演講、寫文章，都喜歡用 *First*，*Second*，*Third*，*Finally*，*In conclusion* 等轉承語，把整篇演講稿或文章串聯起來。並不一定要用老套，也可以把 *First* 改成 *Firstly* 或 *First of all*，*To begin with*，或 *To start with*，甚至用 *For starters*，*For openers*，*For one thing* 等。

　　凡是作文想不出來，接下來該怎麼寫的時候，就可以用 *Next*，*Also*，*Again* 或 *What's more*，*Moreover*，*Furthermore*；想要強調什麼事的時候，可以用 *In fact*，*In reality*，*In actuality* 等。要解釋前面所說的話時，就可以說 *That is to say* 之類的。舉例說明時，可以說：*For example*，*For instance*，*Take…for example*. 或 *Take…as an example*. 同學只要會寫英文句子（不會寫就背「一口氣背會話」），再背了轉承語，就很會寫作文了。

　　「如何寫英文作文」從頭到尾把英文作文該怎麼寫，敘述得一清二楚，言簡意賅。從標題、主題句、推展句，到結尾句，加上最完整的轉承語，並附上歷屆學測、指考試題來驗證。

　　本書由謝靜芳老師實際上過課，也經過多次校對，仍恐有疏漏之處，尚祈同學們不吝批評指正。

劉毅

CONTENTS

UNIT 1 英作文轉承語總整理

背了下列轉承語，就會寫英文作文：（增訂自「一口氣背同義字寫作文」）

Track 1

I. 表示次序或時間

1.
First 首先	**At first** 最初
= Firstly	= Initially
= First of all	= Originally
	= At the outset
= In the first place	
= To begin with	= At the beginning
= To start with	= From the beginning
	= From the start
= For starters	
= For openers	
= For one thing	

2.
Second 第二	= Later
= In the second place	= Later on
Third 第三	
= In the third place	= After a while
	= Following that
Then 然後	
= **Next** 其次	= By and by
	= Subsequently
= **Afterward(s)** 之後	
= After this	**Soon** 很快
= Thereafter	= Shortly
	= Presently

UNIT 1

= In a minute
= In a second

= In a short while
= In a short time

= In the near future
= Before long

At the same time 同時
= At the same instant
= In the same breath

= All at once
= All together

= Simultaneously
= Concurrently

3.
What's more 此外
= More
= Moreover

= In addition
= Additionally
= Plus

= Over and above that
= Furthermore
= Again

= Besides
= Besides that
= On top of that

4.
Finally 最後
= Finally, but most
   importantly
= Last but not least
   最後但並非最不重要的

= At last
= At long last
= At length

= Ultimately
= Eventually

= Last
= Lastly
= Last and most
   importantly

= In the end
= In the long run

= Most importantly
= Most of all
= Most important of all

= Above all
= After all
= All things considered

5.
In conclusion 總之	= Shortly
= In summary	= Briefly
= In sum	= Concisely
= In closing	
= In short 簡言之	= To put it briefly
= In brief	= To put it simply
= In a word	= Simply put
= To conclude	= In all
= To sum up	= All in all
= To summarize	= Overall
	= Altogether

6.
In general 大體上	= As a whole
= Generally speaking	= On the whole
	= For the most part
= Essentially	
= Fundamentally	= As a rule 通常
	= As usual
= By and large	= Ordinarily
= At large	

II. 表示因果關係

Track 2

1.
In this way 這樣一來	= Accordingly
= For this reason	= Consequently
= Because of this	
= As a result	= Therefore
= As a consequence	= Thereupon
= In consequence	= Hence
	= Thus 因此；所以；於是；結果

UNIT 1

Ⅲ. 表示舉例或例證

  Track 3

1.
{ **For example** 例如
{ = For instance
{ = e.g.

{ = By way of example
{ = As an example

{ = Take…for example
{ = Take…as an example
{   以…為例
{ 【不可用 instance 代替
{   example】

{ = As an illustration
{ = To illustrate
{ = To demonstrate

Ⅳ. 表示比較或對比

  Track 4

1.
{ **However** 然而
{ = Yet
{ = Still

{ = But then
{ = Then again
{ = For all that
{ = After all

{ = Nevertheless
{ = Nonetheless
{ = On the other hand

{ Meanwhile 同時
{ = In the meantime
{ = At the same time

{ = In spite of this
{ = Despite this
{ = Even so

{ While this may be true
{ 雖然這可能是真的
{ = Be that as it may

2.
{ **Conversely** 相反地
{ = On the contrary
{ = Contrarily

{ = Instead
{ = Rather

3. **In contrast** 對比之下
  = By contrast
  = By way of contrast

4. **Ironically** 諷刺地
  = Paradoxically
  = Absurdly

V. 表示強調

Track 5

1. **In fact** 事實上
  = In effect
  = In truth

  = In reality
  = In actuality

  = As a matter of fact
  = In point of fact
  = Indeed

  = Actually
  = Truly

  = Honestly
  = Frankly

  = To tell the truth
  = To be honest
  = To be frank

  = Regarding this
  = Considering this

2. **Equally** 同樣地
  = Similarly
  = Likewise

  = In the same way
  = In the same manner
  = In like manner

  = In a similar fashion
  = By the same token
  = Equally important

3. **Of course** 當然
  = As a matter of course
  = Surely
  = To be sure

  = Indeed 的確
  = No doubt 無疑地
  = Without (a) doubt

= Undoubtedly	= Naturally　當然
= Certainly	= Obviously
= Granted	= Needless to say

4.
In other words　也就是說	= Namely
= That is	= To put it another way
= That is to say	= To put it differently

5.
By the way　順便一提	= Parenthetically
= Incidentally	= Apropos〔͵æprə'po〕
= To change the topic	= By the bye

6.
Especially　特別；尤其	= Particularly
= Specifically	= In particular
	= Notably

7.
In any case　無論如何	= Anyhow
= In any event	= Anyway
= At any rate	
	= Whatever the case may be
	= Whatever happens

8.
Regrettably　可惜；遺憾地	= Unluckily
= As a matter of regret	= Unhappily
= Unfortunately	= Sadly

9.
Strangely enough　真奇怪	= Curiously enough
= Oddly enough	= Strange to say
= Bizarrely enough	= Surprisingly

UNIT 2 英文寫作法的基本原則 ✐

I. 題目的寫法

1. 題目要居中。

【例 1】

My Favorite Color

〔主題句〕Gray is my favorite color for several reasons. 〔推展句①〕*First*, it's a neutral color: in terms of clothing, gray goes with everything. 〔推展句②〕*Second*, it always gives me a pleasant feeling to see the color gray. It soothes me. 〔推展句③〕*Lastly*, gray is the color of the sky when it rains, and I love rainy days. There's something very relaxing about the sound of the rain, and it helps me sleep. 〔結尾句〕Sleeping is one of my favorite activities; *thus*, the color gray is an important part of my life.

【例 2】

How to Break Bad Habits

〔主題句〕Bad habits disrupt your life. They prevent you from accomplishing your goals. They jeopardize your health both mentally and physically. And bad habits waste your time and energy. *Therefore*, it is important to understand them.

〔推展句①〕*First of all*, recognizing the causes of your bad habits is crucial to overcoming them. *Most of the time*, bad habits are simply a way of dealing with stress and boredom. Everything from biting your nails to wasting time on the Internet can be a response to stress and boredom. 〔推展句②〕Because bad habits provide some type of benefit in your life, it's very difficult to simply eliminate them. *Instead*, you need to replace a bad habit with a new habit that provides a similar benefit.

〔結尾句〕*Fortunately*, you can teach yourself new and healthy ways to deal with stress and boredom, which you can then substitute in place of your bad habits.

2. **第一個字、重要的字首要大寫**，但冠詞、介詞（4個字母以下）、
連接詞小寫。例如：

A Horrible Experience
（一個可怕的經驗）

The Importance of Etiquette
（禮儀的重要性）

The Most Precious Thing in My Room
（我房裡最珍貴的東西）

Music Is an Important Part of Life
（音樂是生活中很重要的一部份）

The Typhoon（颱風）

Clothes Make the Man（人要衣裝）

Whether High School Students Should Wear Uniforms
（高中生是否應該穿制服）

The Most Unforgettable Person in My Life
（我一生中最難忘的人）

Democracy（民主政治）

A Romantic Surprise（爛漫的驚喜）

A Letter to a Friend on His Birthday
（給朋友的生日賀函）

To Learn from Failure（從失敗中學習）

Money Is Not Everything（金錢不是一切）

自我測驗　請用正確的大小寫字體訂正下列的作文題目：

1. pride goes before a fall

   _____

2. why I want to attend college

   _____

3. laughter is better than medicine

   _____

4. the person who influenced me most

   _____

5. eating in Taiwan

   _____

6. if I had magic power

   _____

7. helping others is the root of happiness

   _____

8. never put off till tomorrow what you can do today

   _____

9. knowledge is power

   _____

10. money isn't everything

   _____

UNIT 2

UNIT 2

11. health is better than wealth

_____

12. what I want to do most after the college entrance exam

_____

13. the country I want to visit most

_____

14. the most unforgettable experience

_____

15. city life and country life

_____

16. if I were an English teacher

_____

17. how to overcome your laziness

_____

18. don't give up halfway

_____

19. a sense of humor

_____

20. honesty is the best policy

_____

3. 不要標點符號，但問號和感嘆號例外。

例如： How to Achieve Success（成功之道）

An Invitation to Visit Taiwan（邀請訪問台灣）

What Makes a Good Friend?
（好朋友該具備什麼條件？）

II. 段落的組成

每一個段落只能有一個主題（central idea），表達主題的句子稱為主題句（topic sentence）。其餘的句子都是在說明或支持這個主旨的推展句。最後作總結的句子稱為結尾句（concluding sentence）。

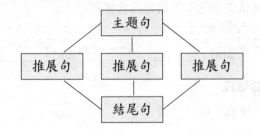

1. 每段開頭空 5 或 7 個字母。

2. 推展句要 3 個以上。

〔主題句〕*Slavery in the United States existed almost unchanged for 100 years.* 〔推展句 1〕During this time, most slaves were not allowed to marry or to raise families. 〔推展句 2〕Usually they were not allowed to learn to read. 〔推展句 3〕It was very dangerous for a slave to travel since even free Negroes could be kidnapped（綁架）and sold at any time. 〔結尾句〕*Under these conditions, it was almost impossible for them to organize to help each other.*

Ⅲ. 如何寫主題句

1. 用題目的關鍵字造句。

2. 句子要簡潔，最好是簡單句。

比較： In my opinion, there are some steps which everybody knows we must take to achieve success.

（太長，複雜，不能寫推展句）

We must take some steps to *achieve success*.

（簡潔，易接轉承語）

Ⅳ. 如何寫推展句

1. 用轉承語引導推展句。

2. 儘量以單句、合句、複句混合使用。

    ☐. ☐. ☐. ☐. ✕（太單調）

    ☐ and ☐. ☐ and ☐. ✕

Ⅴ. 結尾句的組成

1. 用表「結論」的轉承語。

2. 把握主題句的關鍵字。

In conclusion, if we follow these steps, we will *achieve success*.

UNIT 3 123寫作法 ✎

1. 大部份的文章都可以用 First, …. Second, …. Third, …. Finally, …. In conclusion, …. 逐條說明。

2. 爲了使文章生動，First 可用 First of all, In the first place, To begin with 等同義轉承語代替。

3. Second 可用 Then, Next 等代替。

4. 其他可用 What's more, Moreover, Furthermore 等代替。

UNIT 2

【萬用作文 1】

The Keys to Achieving Success

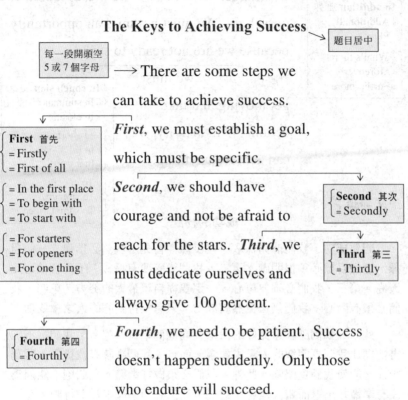

題目居中

每一段開頭空
5 或 7 個字母

→ There are some steps we can take to achieve success.

First, we must establish a goal, which must be specific.

First 首先
= Firstly
= First of all

= In the first place
= To begin with
= To start with

= For starters
= For openers
= For one thing

Second, we should have courage and not be afraid to reach for the stars. *Third*, we must dedicate ourselves and always give 100 percent.

Second 其次
= Secondly

Third 第三
= Thirdly

Fourth, we need to be patient. Success doesn't happen suddenly. Only those who endure will succeed.

Fourth 第四
= Fourthly

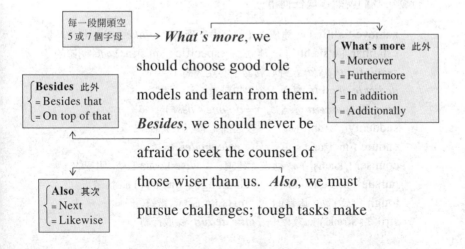

每一段開頭空
5 或 7 個字母

→ *What's more*, we should choose good role models and learn from them. *Besides*, we should never be afraid to seek the counsel of those wiser than us. *Also*, we must pursue challenges; tough tasks make

What's more 此外
= Moreover
= Furthermore

= In addition
= Additionally

Besides 此外
= Besides that
= On top of that

Also 其次
= Next
= Likewise

UNIT 3

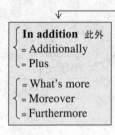

In addition 此外
= Additionally
= Plus

= What's more
= Moreover
= Furthermore

us stronger. *In addition*, we must prepare ourselves. We must not miss an opportunity because we are not ready to strike.

In conclusion, we must get moving and take action. With activity, we can achieve anything.

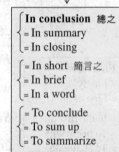

In conclusion 總之
= In summary
= In closing

= In short 簡言之
= In brief
= In a word

= To conclude
= To sum up
= To summarize

【中文翻譯】

成功的秘訣

　　想要成功，我們能夠採取一些步驟。首先，我們必須建立一個目標，這個目標必須很明確。第二，我們應該要有勇氣，不要害怕心比天高。第三，我們必須要專心，一定要盡自己最大的努力。第四，我們必須有耐心。我們無法突然就成功。只有堅持到底的人才會成功。

　　此外，我們應該選擇好的榜樣，向他們學習。還有，我們絕不能害怕向比我們更明智的人尋求建議。而且，我們應該尋找挑戰；艱難的任務能使我們更堅強。此外，我們必須做好準備。我們絕不能因為沒有準備好出擊而錯失機會。總之，我們必須站起來採取行動。有了行動，我們就能達成任何事。

　　* achieve〔ə'tʃiv〕v. 達成；（經努力）獲得　　*take steps* 採取步驟
　　establish〔ə'stæblɪʃ〕v. 建立　　specific〔spɪ'sɪfɪk〕adj. 明確的
　　reach for the stars 野心勃勃；心比天高
　　dedicate oneself 專心；全力以赴
　　give 100 percent 盡全力（= *do one's best*）
　　suddenly〔'sʌdn̩lɪ〕adv. 一夜之間；忽然；突然
　　endure〔ɪn'dʒʊr〕v. 堅持　　*role model* 榜樣
　　counsel〔'kaʊnsl̩〕n. 勸告；建議　　wise〔waɪz〕adj. 明智的
　　pursue〔pɚ'su〕v. 尋求　　challenge〔'tʃælɪndʒ〕n. 挑戰
　　tough〔tʌf〕adj. 困難的　　miss〔mɪs〕v. 錯過
　　strike〔straɪk〕v. 攻擊　　*take action* 採取行動

【萬用作文 2】

Take a Trip to Taiwan

日期在第一行，
齊右邊

May. 10, 2017

Dear Chloe,

稱呼語在第二
行，齊左邊，
須用逗點

每一段開頭空
5 或 7 個字母

What's new? I strongly

suggest you pay a visit to Taiwan.

To begin with, the weather here is

fantastic. It's not too hot in the summer

and it's not too cold in the winter.

It's a pleasant climate. *Also*,

Taiwanese are so warm and

welcoming, especially to visitors.

Young and old, rich and poor, from any

nation—all are welcome in Taiwan.

To begin with 首先
= To start with
= In the first place

= First
= Firstly
= First of all

= For starters
= For openers
= For one thing

Also 其次
= In addition

每一段開頭空
5 或 7 個字母

Everybody knows that Taiwan

is paradise for food lovers. All kinds

of Chinese cuisine are on offer.

Whatever dish you desire, you can find

it in Taiwan. Have you ever tried baked

buns, fried dough sticks, or soybean

milk? That's a typical Chinese

**Everybody knows
that** 大家都知道
= We all know that

breakfast. I have no doubt you will like it. ***Besides***, Taipei is a city that never sleeps. I can take you to a night market, where we can feast on tasty snacks, such as oyster omelets, stinky tofu, pig blood cakes, pig blood soup, and bubble tea. Everyone should try chicken feet, even if they sound unusual.

Besides 此外
= Besides that
= On top of that

= What's more
= Moreover
= Furthermore

= In addition
= Additionally
= Also

In addition, I can take you to Yangming Mountain for hiking and bathing in the hot springs. ***After that***,

In addition 此外
= Additionally
= Also

= Besides
= Besides that
= On top of that

= What's more
= Moreover
= Furthermore

After that 之後
= Then

we can tour Taipei 101, Chiang Kai-shek Memorial Hall, and the National Palace Museum.

每一段開頭空
5 或 7 個字母 ⟶ Taiwan has traditional Chinese culture, but a modern, high tech society. ***In fact***, Taiwan is a combination of East and West. ***Here***, everyone can find something to enjoy. Travelers, shoppers, and food lovers all adore Taiwan.

In fact 事實上
= In reality
= Indeed

= As a matter of fact
= Actually
= Truly

Here 在這裡
= Here in Taiwan
= In Taiwan 在台灣

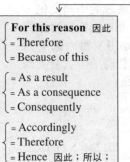

For this reason 因此
= Therefore
= Because of this

= As a result
= As a consequence
= Consequently

= Accordingly
= Therefore
= Hence　因此；所以；
　於是；結果

For this reason, I am inviting you now, so start making plans. Let me know the date and time. I will meet you at the airport. *Of course*, it's my pleasure to make all the arrangements. All you have to do is (to) show up.

Of course 當然
= Surely
= To be sure

結尾敬詞
須加逗點

Your friend,

Bill

簽名在最後一行，
結尾敬詞的下方

UNIT 3

【中文翻譯】

去台灣旅行

親愛的克洛伊：

　　最近如何？我強烈建議妳來台灣玩。首先，台灣的天氣很棒，夏天不會太熱，冬天也不會太冷。這裡的天氣令人愉快。此外，台灣人很親切又熱情，尤其是對觀光客。無論男女老少、不分貧富，不管你來自哪一國——在台灣全都會受到歡迎。

　　大家都知道，台灣是美食者的天堂。各種中式料理在這裡都買得到。無論你想要吃什麼菜，在台灣都找得到。妳有試過燒餅、油條，或豆漿嗎？這是中式早餐，我確信你會很喜歡。此外，台北是個不夜城。我可以帶妳去夜市，在那裏我們能大啖美味的點心，像是蚵仔煎、臭豆腐、豬血糕、豬血湯、泡沫紅茶；雞腳是每個人都該品嚐的東西，雖然聽起來很不尋常。另外，我可以帶妳去陽明山爬山和泡溫泉。之後，我們可以去參觀台北101大樓、中正紀念堂，以及國立故宮博物院。

事實上，台灣融合了中西方文化。台灣有傳統的中國文化，也是個現代化高科技的城市。在這裡，每個人都可以找到喜歡的東西。遊客、購物者，以及美食愛好者，全都很喜歡台灣。因此，我現在要邀請你開始計畫。讓我知道日期和時間，我會去機場接你。當然，這是我的榮幸。妳只要人來就好。

你的朋友，
比爾
2017 年 5 月 10 日

* ***What's new?*** 有什麼新鮮事；最近如何？
suggest〔səg'dʒɛst〕*v.* 建議
fantastic〔fæn'tæstɪk〕*adj.* 很棒的
pleasant〔'plɛzn̩t〕*adj.* 令人愉快的
welcoming〔'wɛlkəmɪŋ〕*adj.* 熱情的
especially〔ə'spɛʃəlɪ〕*adv.* 尤其；特別是
young and old 無論老少；不分男女老幼
rich and poor 有錢人和窮人　　paradise〔'pærə,daɪz〕*n.* 天堂
cuisine〔kwɪ'zin〕*n.* 菜餚　　***on offer*** 出售中
desire〔dɪ'zaɪr〕*v.* 慾望；想要
baked bun 燒餅　　***fried dough stick*** 油條（= *Chinese fritter*）

soybean milk 豆漿　　typical〔'tɪpɪkl̩〕*adj.* 典型的
have no doubt 毫不懷疑；確信　　***night market*** 夜市
feast on 品嚐；大吃大喝　　tasty〔'testɪ〕*adj.* 好吃的
snack〔snæk〕*n.* 點心　　***oyster omelet*** 蚵仔煎
stinky tofu 臭豆腐　　***pig blood cake*** 豬血糕
pig blood soup 豬血湯　　bubble〔'bʌbl̩〕*n.* 泡泡
bubble tea 泡沫紅茶　　unusual〔ʌn'juʒʊəl〕*adj.* 不尋常的
hiking〔'haɪkɪŋ〕*n.* 爬山　　bathe〔beð〕*v.* 洗澡；沐浴
hot spring 溫泉　　***Chiang Kei-shek Memorial Hall*** 中正紀念堂

the National Palace Museum 國立故宮博物院
traditional〔trə'dɪʃənl̩〕*adj.* 傳統的　　***high tech*** 高科技的
combination〔,kɑmbə'neʃən〕*n.* 組合　　adore〔ə'dor〕*v.* 非常喜愛
make plans 做計畫　　***make arrangements*** 做安排
It's my pleasure. 這是我的榮幸。
all one has to do is (to) V. 某人所要做的就是…　　***show up*** 出現

UNIT 3

文意選填

【**Test 1**】

> 說明：第1題至第20題，每題一個空格，請依文意在文章後所提供的 (A) 到 (U) 選項中分別選出最適當者，並將其英文字母代號畫記在答案卡之「選擇題答案區」。各題答對者，得5分；答錯、未作答者，該題以零分計算。

How to Achieve Success

We must take some steps to achieve success. ___1___, we must set a goal, which must be clear-cut. Second, we should have confidence ___2___ not be afraid to dream big dreams. ___3___, we must commit ourselves and always make our best effort. Fourth, we need to be patient. Success doesn't happen ___4___. Only those who persist will succeed.

What's more, we should select good ___5___ and learn from them. ___6___, we should never be afraid to ask others for advice. Also, we must ___7___ challenges; tough tasks make us stronger. In addition, we must be ready. We must not miss a chance ___8___ we are unprepared. ___9___, we must get on our feet and take action. ___10___ action, we can achieve anything.

(A) With	(B) role models
(C) First	(D) overnight
(E) and	(F) because
(G) Besides	(H) In conclusion
(I) Third	(J) It is thought that
(K) seek	(L) In

【Test 2】

An Invitation to Visit Taiwan

Jan. 19, 2017

Dear Jimmy,

How are you doing? I highly recommend you visit Taiwan. ___11___, the weather here is great. It's not too hot in the summer and it's not too cold in the winter. It's a healthy climate. ___12___, Taiwanese are so friendly, especially to visitors. Young and old, rich and poor, from any nation—all are welcome.

___13___ Taiwan is a gourmet's paradise. All kinds of Chinese cuisine are available. Whatever dish you like, you can find it in Taiwan. Have you ever tried baked buns, fried dough sticks, or soybean milk? That's a typical Chinese breakfast. I am sure you will like it. Besides, Taipei is a city ___14___ never sleeps. I can take you to a night market, where we can sample tasty snacks, such as oyster omelets, stinky tofu, pig blood cakes, pig blood soup and bubble tea. Chicken feet are something everyone should try, even if they sound frightening. In ___15___, I can take you to Yangming Mountain for hiking and hot springs.

___16___, we can visit Taipei 101, Chiang Kai-shek Memorial Hall, and the National Palace Museum.

Taiwan has traditional Chinese culture, but a modern, high tech society. ___17___, Taiwan is a mix of East and West. ___18___, there is something for everyone. Travelers, shoppers, and food lovers all adore Taiwan.

___19___ a result, I am inviting you now, so please make it happen. Just tell me the date and time. I will pick you up at the airport. Of course, I will be happy to make all the arrangements. ___20___ you have to do is show up.

Your friend,

Johnny

UNIT 3

(A) Here in Taiwan   (B) In fact

(C) To begin with   (D) Also

(E) We all know that   (F) addition

(G) that   (H) After that

(I) contrast   (J) For

(K) For another   (L) In comparison

(M) As   (N) All

(O) Whatever   (P) No matter what

(Q) On the contrary   (R) As the saying goes

UNIT 4 如何寫主題句

1. 主題句爲該段所要描述的或説明的主旨，爲一完整的句子，盡量使用簡單句，或簡潔的句子。

比較：

① *Pride and Prejudice* was a book which in my opinion I enjoyed reading very much. (傲慢與偏見，在我看來，是我很喜歡讀的一本書。)【差，複雜不清楚】

② I enjoyed reading *Pride and Prejudice*. (我很喜歡讀傲慢與偏見。)【佳，直接明瞭】

【範例】

題目：將來完成學業之後，你想從事哪一種職業？

〔主題句〕*The field that I plan to enter is nursing.* 〔推展句①〕This occupation is one that is essential in any society. People will always get ill or become injured and need someone to care for them. Helping others gives me a great deal of satisfaction, and that is why I believe I will feel fulfilled as a nurse. 〔推展句②〕*In addition*, there will be many opportunities to specialize within this field, *for example*, as a pediatric nurse or an emergency room nurse. 〔結論句〕*Therefore*, I can pursue my own interests *while* serving society at the same time.

我想進入的領域是護理工作。這個職業在任何社會都很重要。人們一定會生病或受傷，需要有人照顧他們。幫助別人使我感到非常滿足，這也是爲什麼我覺得自己會在護士這一行中得到成就。除此之外，在這個領域中，有很多機會可以專攻某個科別，例如成爲小兒科護士，或是一位急診室護士。因此，我可以在服務社會的同時，追求自己的興趣。

【範例 ②】

〔主題句〕*The Spartathlon's attraction has two sources*. 〔推展句①〕*The first* is the difficulty of finishing it. The Spartathlon is not the most difficult race, but it combines lots of different tests. There is the heat of the Greek day, and then the plunge in temperature when darkness falls. There are climbs: the route includes a series of ascents, among them a 1,200-meter mountain pass in the dead of night. *Above all*, there is the relentless pressure of the clock. 〔推展句②〕*The second reason* is that the idea of retracing Pheidippides's footsteps still grips many participants. It feels like racing in history, passing through places where history began. (102 年指考)

UNIT 4

斯巴達松吸引人的原因有兩點。第一點是它很難完成。斯巴達松並非最困難的賽跑，但它結合了許多困難的考驗。有希臘白天炎熱，當黑夜降臨時，氣溫卻驟降。有許多的爬坡，此路徑涵蓋了一連串的上坡，其中包括了在深夜時候，通過一段1200公尺的山路。尤其是時間的無情壓力。第二個理由是，追循著費底皮斯的腳步，這樣的構想仍舊吸引了許多參加者。感覺就像是在歷史中賽跑，經過了歷史起源的地方。

2. 利用提供的詞語，選出最可能的主題句。

【例 1 】 Fever, chills, persistent cough

    (A) These are reasons to go to schorl.

    (B) These are reasons to see a doctor.

    (C) These are reasons to sleep late.

    (D) These are reasons to fail a test.

【例 2】 Thriller, romantic comedy, science fiction

    (A) These are socially acceptable forms of behavior.

    (B) These are three types of movie.

    (C) These are types of addiction.

    (D) These are metropolitan areas.

【例 3】 Pace of life, job opportunities, noise level

    (A) These are the goals of going to college.

    (B) These are differences between city life and country life.

    (C) These are the purposes of leaving home.

    (D) These are the things your parents won't do for you.

【例 4】 Drinking and driving, cancer, heart disease

    (A) These are the leading causes of death.

    (B) These are the most popular forms of adult entertainment.

    (C) These are the best tourist destinations in Asia.

    (D) These are the only things that can kill you.

【例 5】 Burning fossils fuels, raising cattle, deforestation

    (A) These are the five habits of wealthy people.

    (B) These are the rules of agriculture.

    (C) These are things people usually ignore.

    (D) These are causes of global warming.

【例 6 】 Health, weight loss, social activity

    (A) These are good reasons to break up with your boyfriend.

    (B) These are the most popular forms of adult entertainment.

    (C) These are reasons why people may exercise.

    (D) These are the only things that can kill you.

【例 7 】 Buy seeds and potting soil, plant seeds, water soil

    (A) These are the steps in growing flowers.

    (B) These are things covered in the newspaper.

    (C) These are things people frequently complain about.

    (D) These are things that cause an earthquake.

【例 8 】 Knowledge, patience, kindness

    (A) These are reasons to go to church.

    (B) These are reasons to see a doctor.

    (C) These are the characteristics of a good doctor.

    (D) These are reasons to wake up early.

【例 9 】 Money, fame, fun lifestyle

    (A) These are shoe styles.

    (B) These are fashion icons.

    (C) These are advantages of being a celebrity.

    (D) These are ethnicities.

UNIT 4

3. 使用關鍵字來寫主題句，以此貫串全文。

① 題目：誤會（Misunderstandings）

主題句： A *misunderstanding* is like an infectious disease.

（誤會就像傳染病一樣。）

② 題目：酸雨（Acid Rain）

主題句： Our environment has suffered from the effects of *acid rain*.

（我們的環境因酸雨所產生的影響而受到損害。）

【範例 ①】

Studying Abroad

〔主題句〕After I graduate from college, I want to *study abroad*. 〔推展句①〕*First*, in this global village, language is not only a necessary skill but also a channel through which I can understand the world better. 〔推展句②〕*Second*, I major in foreign languages in my college life. *Studying abroad* would be a good chance for me to overcome my fear of speaking English. 〔推展句③〕*Last*, *studying abroad* would transform me from a dependent student into an adult who takes charge of his life.

出國唸書

我大學畢業後，想要出國讀書。我要出國讀書有三個原因。第一，在這個地球村裡，語言不只是一項必須的技能，也是一個能更加了解這個世界的途徑。第二，我在大學生活裡主修外語。出國讀書對我而言是個好機會，能使我克服說英文的恐懼。最後，出國讀書將使我由一個依賴的學生，轉變成一個能掌控自己生活的成年人。

【範例 ②】

Keeping an English Diary

〔主題句〕*Keeping a diary in English* has many benefits. 〔推展句①〕*First*, it is fun to have to think in English. It is hard at first, but it gets easier with practice. 〔推展句②〕*Second*, the *diary* gives me a record of my ability. As time goes by, my grammar and vocabulary improve. I enjoy looking back and seeing the progress. 〔推展句③〕*Third*, simply *keeping a diary* gives me a chance to reflect. This would also be true if I wrote in Chinese, but using English requires me to think even more. 〔結論句〕*Finally*, my family would not be able to read my *diary* if they found it. None of them know English, so my secrets are safe in my *English diary*.

寫英文日記

用英文寫日記有很多好處。首先,必須用英文思考很有趣。剛開始很難,但是越練習,就變得越簡單。其次,日記能讓我記錄自己的能力。隨著時間的過去,我的文法和字彙都進步了。我喜歡回顧過去,看看自己進步的情況。第三,單單寫日記,就能讓我有機會反省。如果我用中文寫日記,也是做得到這一點,但是用英文寫,我就必須想得更多。最後,我的家人如果發現我的日記,他們也看不懂。他們沒有人懂英文,所以我的秘密可以安全地保存在我的英文日記裡。

4. 利用關鍵字，寫出以下各篇文章標題可能的主題句。

【例 1】題目：A Graduation Ceremony

〔主題句〕 _____.

【例 2】題目：An Unforgettable Exam

〔主題句〕 _____.

【例 3】題目：Travel Is the Best Teacher

〔主題句〕 _____.

【例 4】題目：Bullying

〔主題句〕 _____.

【例 5】題目：A World Without Electricity

〔主題句〕 _____.

【例 6】題目：An Activity for the Graduates

〔主題句〕 _____.

【例 7】題目：On Being Misunderstood

〔主題句〕 _____.

【例 8】題目：An Impressive Commercial

〔主題句〕 _____.

【例 9】題目：An Unforgettable Smell

〔主題句〕 _____.

【例 10】題目：Our Lives with TV

〔主題句〕 _____.

UNIT 4

【例11】題目：Insomnia

　　〔主題句〕 _____ .

【例12】題目：Laziness

　　〔主題句〕 _____ .

【例13】題目：On Honesty

　　〔主題句〕 _____ .

【例14】題目：On Cooperation

　　〔主題句〕 _____ .

【例15】題目：My Mother

　　〔主題句〕 _____ .

【例16】題目：How I Spend Sundays

　　〔主題句〕 _____ .

【例17】題目：Money

　　〔主題句〕 _____ .

【例18】題目：My Motto

　　〔主題句〕 _____ .

【例19】題目：Night Markets

　　〔主題句〕 _____ .

【例20】題目：A Sense of Responsibility

　　〔主題句〕 _____ .

UNIT 4

5. 試寫出以下各篇文章的主題句。

【例 1 】

〔主題句〕_____.

My *first* visit was in the summer of 1964, to see the World's Fair. *The second time* was in 1966, to see friends. *The last time* I visited New York was just last month, when I went there to look for a job. Maybe soon I will be a resident of New York instead of a visitor.

【例 2 】

〔主題句〕_____.

When he was only a freshman in high school, he played on the varsity team. Throughout high school, he scored an average of twenty-six points a game. *Then* he was given a basketball scholarship to college. Now people think that Bob has a good chance of becoming a professional someday.

【例 3 】

〔主題句〕_____.

The first step is to cut out a pattern on a flat block of wood. *Second*, spread printer's ink over the surface of the wood block. *Third*, press the inked block against a sheet of paper. When the ink has dried on the paper, your woodcut is finished.

【例4】

〔主題句〕＿＿＿＿＿＿＿＿＿＿＿＿＿＿＿＿＿＿＿＿＿.

This is done with an instrument which allows doctors to see a baby while it is still in the mother. Such examinations before birth may eventually decrease the number of children who die in their first year of life.

【例5】

〔主題句〕＿＿＿＿＿＿＿＿＿＿＿＿＿＿＿＿＿＿＿＿＿.

His eyes were bloodshot and teary. His hands shook when he lit a cigarette, and he coughed incessantly. *Finally*, his wife persuaded him to see a doctor.

【例6】

〔主題句〕＿＿＿＿＿＿＿＿＿＿＿＿＿＿＿＿＿＿＿＿＿.

Although the summer sun can be a wicked fireball sometimes, I like it none the less for it. Ice cream in summer is the tops. Whenever I come across an ice cream parlor during summer, I can't help but eat ice cream to my heart's delight.

【例7】

〔主題句〕＿＿＿＿＿＿＿＿＿＿＿＿＿＿＿＿＿＿＿＿＿.

We must keep our community neat and clean. We should always dispose of our garbage properly. We should be considerate of our neighbors. Living in such a crowded place, we should keep in mind our neighbor's right to peace and quiet. If we can all do these things, I'm sure our community will be a better place to live in.

【例 8】

〔主題句〕 _____.

Everybody needs friends. A friend is someone who is there
to help you get through the rough times. A friend is someone
who keeps you company and someone you can confide in.
In order to make friends, you have to reach out your hands
first before anything else. *Indeed*, no one can live alone.

【例 9】

〔主題句〕 _____.

Books are like friends. They can comfort us and help us.
Unlike friends though, they will always be there whenever
we need them. Books are also like tools we can use. The
information and knowledge they contain can open new doors
for us. It is difficult to imagine a life without books.

【例 10】

〔主題句〕 _____.

Keeping healthy and fit is a duty we owe ourselves. In this
busy world it is harder and harder to find time to get some
exercise. I find that a half-hour jog in the morning before I go
to work fits into my schedule well. I feel good the whole day.
If you don't like to jog, then a simple brisk walk has a similar
effect. *So* grab a friend and jog or walk through the park.

【作文範例 ①】

提示： 全球暖化已不只是報紙上的國際新聞，節能減碳抗暖化已是當務之急，你我隨手一個簡單的小動作，就能有效減少二氧化碳的排放，挽救暖化的日漸惡化。請以 "How to Slow Global Warming" (如何減緩全球暖化的速度) 爲題，寫一篇短文，以你個人的角度，提供生活上的小撇步。

How to Slow Global Warming

〔主題句〕*There are many tangible steps we can take in order to slow global warming*. We should spare no effort to do the following things. 〔推展句①〕*First*, we can reduce our use of air-conditioners by using fans and opening the windows instead. 〔推展句②〕*Secondly*, we can form a group for the purpose of planting trees. Every person in the group would have the responsibility of taking care of the trees he planted. Little by little, the number of trees would grow, and the environment would improve. 〔推展句③〕*Last but not least*, we should strive to educate the public on the importance of slowing global warming. Then more people will be willing to participate in conservation efforts. 〔結尾句〕We should look after the environment for the sake of our future generations.

UNIT 4

如何減緩全球暖化的速度

要減緩全球暖化的速度，我們可以採取許多確實可行的步驟。我們應該不遺餘力地做下列的事情。首先，我們可以使用電風扇並開窗戶，以減少使用冷氣。其次，我們可以組成以種樹爲目的的團體。團

體中的每個人，都要負責照顧自己所種的樹。漸漸地，樹木的數
量會增加，環境就會因而改善。最後一項要點是，我們應該努力
教育大衆了解減緩全球暖化的重要性。那就會有更多人願意爲環
保貢獻心力。我們應該爲了後代子孫好好照顧環境！

【作文範例 ②】

提示： 請寫一段有關你心目中的好學生的英文作文，說明你認爲的好
學生的定義爲何，應該具備甚麼樣的特質。

〔主題句〕I believe *there are three distinct qualities or characteristics which define a good student*. 〔推展句①〕
First, a good student must have the faculty of discernment.
He must be able to tell the difference between right and
wrong. This ability, however, often comes from home;
parents help define a child's sense of justice. 〔推展句②〕
Second, a good student should have high moral standards,
which again, usually come down from the parents. 〔推展
句③〕*Finally*, a good student must be open-minded
enough to realize that humility and respect are valuable
characteristics. 〔結尾句〕A good student knows the
potential exists to learn something from every person he
meets.

　　我認爲有三個明確的特質或特徵能給好學生下定義。首先，
好學生必須有洞察力，他們必須能辨別是非。然而這樣的能力通
常來自於家庭，是你的父母親幫你培養正義感。其次，好學生應
該有高道德標準，而這也通常來自於父母親。最後，好學生應該
心胸要夠開闊，能了解謙虛與尊重是珍貴的特質。好學生知道，
從每個遇見的人身上學習的可能性是存在的。

6. 歷屆試題觀摩：

依據的主題句的寫作原則，選出各段落的主題句。

【例 1】

〔主題句〕_____ Fish can "talk" to each other and make a range of noises by vibrating their swim bladder, an internal gas-filled organ used as a resonating chamber to produce or receive sound.

〔主題句〕_____ Damselfish, *for example*, have been found to make sounds to scare off threatening fish and even divers. *Another* discovery about fish sounds is that not all fish are equally "talkative." Some species talk a lot, while others don't. The gurnard species has a wide vocal repertoire and keeps up a constant chatter. Codfish, *on the other hand*, usually keep silent, except when they are laying eggs. Any goldfish lover who hopes to strike up a conversation with their pet goldfish is out of luck. Goldfish have excellent hearing, but they don't make any sound whatsoever. Their excellent hearing isn't associated with vocalization. (102年指考)

(A) Fish are believed to speak to each other for a number of reasons, such as to attract mates, scare off predators, or give directions to other fish.

(B) The undersea world isn't as quiet as we thought, according to a New Zealand researcher.

【例2】

〔主題句〕_____ ***To put it another way***, ads are communication designed to get someone to do something. Even if an advertisement claims to be purely informational, it still has persuasion at its core. The ad informs the consumers with one purpose: to get the consumer to like the brand and, on that basis, to eventually buy the brand. Without this persuasive intent, communication about a product might be news, but it would not be advertising.

〔主題句〕_____ Political advertising is one example. Although political ads are supposed to be concerned with the public welfare, they are paid for and they all have a persuasive intent. They differ from commercial ads in that political ads "sell" candidates rather than commercial goods. A Bush campaign ad, ***for instance***, did not ask anyone to buy anything, yet it attempted to persuade American citizens to view George Bush favorably. ***Aside from*** campaign advertising, political advertising is also used to persuade people to support or oppose proposals. Critics of President Clinton's health care plan used advertising to influence lawmakers and defeat the government's plan.

〔主題句〕_____ ***For instance***, the international organization Greenpeace uses advertising to get their message out. In the ads, they warn people about serious pollution problems and the urgency of protecting the environment. They, too, are selling something and trying to make a point. (101年指考)

(A) Advertising can be persuasive communication not only about a product but also an idea or a person.

(B) All advertising includes an attempt to persuade.

(C) Advertising can be the most important source of income for the media through which it is conducted.

(D) In addition to political parties, environmental groups and human rights organizations also buy advertising to persuade people to accept their way of thinking.

【例 3】

〔主題句〕_____ *In fact*, the Earth receives 20,000 times more energy from the sun than we currently use. If we used more of this source of heat and light, it could supply all the power needed throughout the world.

〔主題句〕_____ *For instance*, many satellites in space are equipped with large panels whose solar cells transform sunlight directly into electric power. These panels are covered with glass and are painted black inside to absorb as much heat as possible.

〔主題句〕_____ *To begin with*, it is a clean fuel.

UNIT 4

In contrast, fossil fuels, such as oil or coal, release harmful substances into the air when they are burned. *What's more*, fossil fuels will run out, but solar energy will continue to reach the Earth long after the last coal has been mined and the last oil well has run dry. (99年指考)

(A) We can harness energy from the sun, or solar energy, in many ways.

(B) Solar energy has a lot to offer.

(C) Solar energy is not earth-friendly at all.

(D) The sun is an extraordinarily powerful source of energy.

【例 4】

〔主題句〕_____ *One* is Rapid Eye Movement (REM) sleep. In this, the brain waves of a sleeping person are similar to those of a waking person, and the eyes move about rapidly under the closed lids. *The other* kind of sleep is Non-Rapid Eye Movement sleep. Scientists have discovered that dreams happen mainly in REM sleep.

〔主題句〕_____ Even people who say they never dream show about 20 percent of REM sleep. If these "non-dreamers" do their sleeping in a laboratory where researchers can wake them up and ask them whether they were having dreams the moment before, it turns out that they dream as much as others.

〔主題句〕_____ *For example*, a boy is having difficulties on the school playground because a bigger boy keeps bullying him. He may dream at night of being alone in the playground, facing a lion. *At other times* the dreaded event from daily life simply occurs in a dream in its real-life form; *that is*, the boy dreams of being bullied by the bigger boy.

〔主題句〕_____ *However*, why a dream will take a certain symbolic form is still a mystery. (89年學測)

(A) Basically, there are two kinds of sleep.
(B) Thanks to scientific research, we learned more about the relationship between sleep and dreams.
(C) Everyone dreams about 20 percent of their sleeping time.
(D) Events in daily life sometimes occur symbolically in dreams.

【例 5】

〔主題句〕_____ Here is an easy way of understanding it. Whenever two people come together, even for a brief moment, they exchange looks, feelings, thoughts, ideas, and energy. Their relationship is how they interact with each other. Everything that happens in the world happens through relationships. We human beings need to love and be loved, and this will come from our relationship with others. *Accordingly*, anyone who wishes to love and be loved will want to establish lasting relationships.

〔主題句〕_____ *First*, we must know our steps. The relationship between two people is like the art of dancing. Before we can dance with a partner, we need to be able to dance by ourselves. We need to feel the rhythm of the music, hear how it inspires us to move and learn our unique style of movement and expression. *Second*, we have to trust. As the key building block for enduring relationships, trust is a bond that evolves as two persons get to know each other and experience safety in opening their hearts. Trust develops when we respect each other's needs and develop a history of common experience and caring. *Third*, we need to be intimate. While intimacy is often limited to the sexual bond, we can be intimate with many people without sexuality, that is, by relating heart to heart. We need to be seen and known by another person. *In this way*, intimacy enables us to thrive and grow.

_____ A new relationship is like an embryo that requires time, care and attention to grow into whatever may evolve. In a proper relationship with others, we will be known and seen for who we are, and love will come out of the seeing and the knowing. (86年學測)

(A) *Lastly*, treat relationship as an organism.

(B) Do you know the meaning of the word "relationship"?

(C) Here are a few tips to help us create enduring relationships.

(D) *Above all*, we must remember out of sight, out of mind.

【例 6】

〔主題句〕 _____ ***In other words***, if you're viewed positively within the critical first four minutes, the person you've met will probably assume everything you do is positive. Give the interviewer a bad impression, and often he will assume you have a lot of unsatisfactory characteristics. ***Worse***, he or she may not take the time to give you a second chance. Most employers believe that those who look as if they care about themselves will care more about their jobs.

（91年北模）

(A) Taking the easy way out is always the best choice.
(B) First impressions are lasting ones.
(C) Nothing good ever comes from making a first impression.

【例 7】

〔主題句〕 _____ ***Type-A*** people are generally considered sensitive perfectionists and good team players, but over-anxious. ***Type Os*** are curious and generous but stubborn. ***Type ABs*** are artistic but mysterious and unpredictable, and type Bs are cheerful but eccentric, individualistic, and selfish. Though lacking scientific evidence, this belief is widely seen in books, magazines, and television shows.

〔主題句〕 _____ The women's softball team that won gold for Japan at the Beijing Olympics is reported to have used blood-type theories to customize training for each player. Some kindergartens have adopted teaching methods along blood group lines, and even major companies reportedly make decisions about assignments based on an employee's blood type. In 1990, Mitsubishi Electronics was reported to have announced the formation of a team composed entirely of AB workers, thanks to "their ability to make plans."

〔主題句〕 _____ One former prime minister considered it important enough to reveal in his official profile that he was a type A, while his opposition rival was type B. In 2011, a minister, Ryu Matsumoto, was forced to resign after only a week in office, when a bad-tempered encounter with local officials was televised. In his resignation speech, he blamed his failings on the fact that he was blood type B.

（105年學測）

(A) The blood-type belief has been used in unusual ways.

(B) The belief even affects politics.

(C) In Japan, a person's blood type is popularly believed to decide his/her temperament and personality.

(D) About 40% of the Japanese population is type A and 30% are type O, whilst only 20% are type B, with AB accounting for the remaining 10%.

UNIT 5 如何寫推展句 ✐

1. 推展句必須支持或說明主題句，試看以下 123 的推展句：

【範例 ①】

〔主題句〕*In my college life, I want to be healthy*.

〔推展句①〕*First of all*, I hope I can avoid the ridiculous life style which many college students pursue. 〔推展句②〕 *Second*, since I will have a lot of free time in college, I want to develop the habit of exercising regularly to keep in shape. 〔推展句③〕*Finally*, I will maintain a healthy diet and get plenty of sleep. 〔結尾句〕*In these ways*, I can live a healthy life in college.

在我的大學生活中，我想要過得健康。首先，我希望我可以避免許多大學生所追求的荒唐生活方式。第二，因為在大學我有很多空閒時間，我想要培養規律運動的習慣，來保持身材。最後，我會維持健康的飲食和有足夠的睡眠。如此一來，我便可以過著健康的大學生活。

【範例 ②】

Whenever a Dalai Lama died, a search began for his reincarnation. 〔主題句〕*The chosen male child had to have certain qualities*. 〔推展句①〕*One* was the ability to identify the belongings of his predecessor, or rather his previous self. 〔推展句②〕*Another* requirement was that he should have large ears, upward-slanting eyes and eyebrows. 〔推展句③〕**Besides**, one of his hands should bear a mark like a conch-shell. 〔結尾句〕The successful candidate, usually aged two or three, was then removed from his family to Lhasa to begin spiritual training for his future role. (93年學測)

　　每當一位達賴喇嘛過世時,就會開始尋找他的轉世喇嘛。被選上的男童,必須具備某些特質。其中一項便是辨別前任喇嘛所有物的能力,或更確切地說,是辨別他自己前身的能力。另一項必備條件是,男童必須具備大耳朵、上揚的眼型及眉毛。此外,有一隻手上得有海螺殼狀的記號。檢驗成功的候選人,通常年齡介於二、三歲之間,得離開家人到拉薩去,爲其未來的角色,接受宗教上的訓練。

2. 常常一句推展句需要較多的解釋,無法一句話就説完,試看以下推展句的發展:

【範例③】

　　〔主題句〕**We can do something to stop our earth from warming up**. 〔推展句①〕**First**, we can take public transportation. 〔推展句①説明〕One bus creates less dirty air than thirty private cars, and it is very convenient to use the bus or MRT in Taipei. 〔推展句②〕**Second**, we can plant more trees. 〔推展句②説明〕Trees are like natural air filters that produce oxygen and energy. 〔推展句③〕**Third**, we can save energy. 〔推展句③説明〕

Generating electricity creates air pollution that leads to rising temperatures, so we should try our very best to cut down on it.

〔結尾句〕*By doing these small things*, we can reduce global warming.

我們還是可以做一些事，阻止地球繼續暖化下去。首先，我們可以搭乘大眾運輸工具。一輛巴士所製造的髒空氣，比三十台私家車輛要少，而且在台北，搭乘公車或捷運是非常方便的。第二，我們可以多種植樹木。樹木就像自然的空氣過濾器，可以製造氧氣並且消除二氧化碳。第三，我們要節省能源。發電製造空氣污染，進而導致氣溫上升，所以我們要盡全力去節約電力的使用。藉由做這些小事情，我們能減少全球暖化。

3. 以下短文，請判斷主題句是否與推展句相關，並找出不相關的主題句或是推展句。

【例 1 】

The old man began to tell us the story of his life. When he was fifteen, he ran away to see the world. He traveled to South America, China, and Australia. When he was too old to work, he came to this country to live with relatives. Now he thinks all the time about the "good old days" when he was young.

是 □

否 □ 不相關的句子：_____

【例 2】

One of the most important men in our society is the
garbage man. Each year more and more garbage is
produced, and more men are required to dispose of it.
These men do this "dirty work" despite the danger of
being disabled or killed by the blades of the disposal
trucks. My brother quit the job because it was too
dangerous. If more people realized how important the
garbage man's job is, perhaps his working conditions
would improve.

是 ☐

否 ☐ 不相關的句子：_____

【例 3】

Spring recess was the best vacation I have ever had. It
rained every single day. Our car broke down three times,
and we spent all our money trying to get it fixed. We
could not afford a place to stay, so we had to sleep in the
car. Then, when we finally gave up and tried to hitchhike
home, we were arrested.

是 ☐

否 ☐ 不相關的句子：_____

【例 4】

Here are the directions to get to my house from yours.
You walk two blocks north and then turn right on Adams
Street. Walk two blocks to the Third Street. My sister
lives at the corner of Adams and Third. Then, turn left on
Third Street and walk until you see a dirt road with a
yellow house on the corner. That is my house.

是 □
否 □ 不相關的句子：_____

【例 5】

It is quite easy to get to Ta An Police Station from your
house. Turn to your right after leaving your house.
Then walk along Hsin Yi Road until you come to Hsin
Sheng South Road. Turn right at the corner of Hsin Sheng
South Road and walk straight. When you come to the corner
of Hsin Sheng South Road and Jen Ai Road, do not cross
the street. Ta An Police Station is at this corner. It is opposite
to the gas station.

是 □
否 □ 不相關的句子：_____

UNIT 5

【例 6】

Stamp collecting is an educational hobby that can be inexpensive and enjoyed whenever you want. It provides a nice and practical way of learning about history, geography, famous people, and customs of various countries worldwide. This hobby began soon after the world saw the first postage stamp issued in Great Britain in 1840. You can *also* get started without spending money by saving the stamps on envelopes you receive. *In addition*, you are able to work on your collection any time, rain or shine. If you are looking for a new hobby, stamp collecting might be right for you!

是 ☐
否 ☐ 不相關的句子：_____

【例 7】

Until relatively recently, people in some parts of the world continued to use salt as a form of cash. There are several reasons why salt was used as money. Salt was given an economic value because there were so few places that produced it in large quantities. *Another* reason is that salt is fairly light and easy to carry for trading purposes. *Additionally*, salt can be measured, so we can easily calculate its value based on its weight. *Furthermore*, salt stays in good condition for a very long period of time, so it holds its value. *Last but not least*, salt has many other uses such as melting ice on roads in snowy regions! *In short*, salt has certain characteristics that make it suitable as a form of money.

是 ☐

否 ☐ 不相關的句子：_____

【例 8】

In the past, most Japanese TV shows started and ended on the hour. While TV shows vary from station to station, *on the whole*, early morning hours are dominated by news programs and evening hours by variety shows. *Because of* competition, some networks tried to gain an advantage over their rivals by starting their programs a little earlier. Many people start channel surfing near the end of a program, and the networks thought that if their show started a couple of minutes earlier, people would start watching it. *Another* strategy was to end a popular show a little after the hour so that people would stick to one channel and miss the beginning of shows on other channels. Now that many stations have adopted these strategies, the advantage for any one station is lost. *Even so*, they continue this practice because they are afraid of losing viewers.

是 □

否 □ 不相關的句子：_____

【例 9】

Trial and error, an approach used in science, is often found in daily life. It can be observed when people do not feel well. They may already have a list of treatments they have used before. They can *also* consult a medical book or check the Internet for new treatments. They may decide to use any one of the treatments. If the treatment does not improve the condition, they try another one. They are concerned about how scientific the treatment is. This is an example of how this approach is adopted in everyday life. In solving problems, scientists come up with more than one idea and use one of the possible options. When an idea fails, they consider the alternatives. *In this way*, approaches used in science and daily life have some points in common.

是 □

否 □ 不相關的句子：_____

UNIT 5

【例10】

Food can do more than fill our stomachs——it also satisfies feelings. If you try to satisfy those feelings with food when you are not hungry, this is known as emotional eating. There are some significant differences between emotional hunger and physical hunger. Emotional and physical hunger are both signals of emptiness, which you try to eliminate with food. Emotional hunger comes on suddenly, while physical hunger occurs gradually. Emotional hunger feels like it needs to be dealt with instantly with the food you want; physical hunger can wait. Emotional eating can leave behind feelings of guilt, but eating due to physical hunger does not. Emotional hunger cannot be fully satisfied with food. Although eating may feel good at that moment, the feeling that caused the hunger is still there.

是 ☐

否 ☐ 不相關的句子：＿＿＿＿＿＿＿＿＿＿＿＿＿＿＿

UNIT 5

II. 段落的組成

1. **用轉承語引導推展句**：轉承語的作用是連結或承轉上下文的語氣，以表示上下文之間的關係。適當使用轉折詞，可使文章更流暢，讀者更可掌握上下文的脈絡。

【範例 ①】

The Advantages of Owning a Business

〔主題句〕*I think owning a business would be better than owning a house*. 〔推展句①〕*First of all*, I would have the opportunity to improve the business and make it more valuable. Usually, the only way to increase the value of a house is to wait for the market to rise and then sell it. 〔推展句②〕*Second*, if I were successful in my business, I would then have enough money to also buy a house. *In this way*, I could have both. 〔推展句③〕*Finally*, I am still young and so can afford to take the risk of choosing a business. 〔結尾句〕*All in all*, owning a business seems like a good idea.

擁有事業的好處

　　我覺得，擁有自己的事業，要比擁有房子更好。首先，我會有機會改善事業，讓它變得更有價值。而通常要讓房價升值的唯一方法，就是等到房價上漲，然後再出售。其次，如果我事業有成，就會有足夠的錢買房子了。這樣一來，我就能兩樣都擁有。最後，我還年輕，可以承擔做生意而不買房子的風險。總之，擁有事業似乎是個不錯的點子。

UNIT 5

【範例 ②】

The Benefits of Class Participation

〔主題句〕*I prefer to participate in class for several reasons.* 〔推展句①〕*One is that* student participation makes the class more lively and interesting. I can hear not only my teacher's opinions on a subject, but also those of my classmates. This often leads to a meaningful discussion. 〔推展句②〕*Another reason is that* I believe the teacher can better understand the students when they interact with him or her in class. Rather than wait for exam results to indicate how much the students have absorbed, the teacher can know immediately whether the students understand what he or she is talking about. 〔推展句③〕*Last but not least*, in my opinion, I can acquire more knowledge in this kind of class. The teacher is a valuable resource, and asking questions in class allows me to make the best use of this resource. I can ask more in-depth questions and satisfy my curiosity. 〔結尾句〕*For these reasons*, I always do my best to participate in class.

UNIT 5

課堂參與的好處

　　我偏愛課堂參與,是基於幾個理由。其中一個原因是,學生的參與讓課堂更有活力,也更有趣。我不但可以聽到老師對某一主題的意見,也可以聽到同學們的看法,如此一來,常會形成一個很有意義的討論。另一原因就是,當學生與老師在課堂上互動時,老師能藉此更加了解學生。老師藉由課堂參與,就能立即知道學生明不明白上課的內容,不用等到測驗結果出來,才知道學生到底吸收了多少。最後一項要點是,在我看來,這種課能讓我獲得更多知識。老師是很寶貴的資源,因此在課堂中發問,我就能充份利用這項資源,並提出更深入的問題,來滿足我的求知慾。

2. 以下短文，請填入適當的轉承語。

【例 1】

    My father is the greatest man that I have ever met. He is a lawyer, and he always appears to be calm and fair. _____, when I have arguments with my brother, my father always settles them fairly. He comes up with a judgment acceptable to both of us; _____, he also shows us what justice is. Because of his influence, I have decided to be a lawyer in the future.

【例 2】

    Hobbies can increase our enjoyment of our lives. We can gain much pleasure by spending time on them. _____, if we waste our time, _____, by drinking or gambling, we not only spoil our lives, but also cause much trouble to others. _____, it is always a good idea to cultivate a good hobby.

【例 3】

    Assuming that I had to travel to a place 40 miles away, I would have a choice of several means of transportation. _____, I could drive my own car, which would give me the greatest flexibility and independence. I could leave at any time I liked and would be able to drive door-to-door. _____, I would have to pay for the gas and for a parking place when I arrived. _____ option would be to take a bus. This would be cheaper but not as comfortable or convenient. I could also take a train. This might cost about the same as a bus, but departures would probably not be as frequent. _____, I could relax on the train and travel in greater comfort. _____, I could ride a motorcycle, but I feel the distance is too great to be comfortable, especially if the weather is bad. Before making a decision, I would have to think about these options carefully.

【例 4】

There are several reasons why perseverance often leads to success. _____, a man who has perseverance does not give up after a failure. He tries again and can, *therefore*, learn from his mistakes. _____, a persistent person is usually a hard worker, and hard work is an important ingredient in success. _____, with perseverance comes a certain amount of confidence—the confidence that one will eventually succeed. *Indeed*, perseverance seems essential to success.

【例 5】

A proverb says: "As you sow, so shall you reap." This proverb is based on the experience of farmers but it is valuable to everyone.

UNIT 5

_____, we must understand that nothing in life is free. _____, we have to work hard for everything we want to get or achieve. The work that we do today will determine whether or not we will be successful tomorrow.

As students, we especially have to remember that we reap what we sow. It follows that we must prepare well for our tests if we want to get good grades. _____, no matter what we do, preparation is the key to our success.

Ⅲ. 1. 儘量以單句、合句、複句混合使用。如此可使句子的關係更清晰，內容更有趣味，有邏輯，不致於太單調。

| ▢▢▢. | ▢▢▢. | ▢▢▢. | ▢▢▢. | × (太單調) |

| ▢▢▢ and ▢▢▢. | ▢▢▢ and ▢▢▢. | × |

比較以下三段文章：

【範例 1-1】

The old man began to tell us the story of his life. He was fifteen. He ran away to sea. He traveled to South America, China, and Australia. Then he was too old to work. He came to this country with relatives. Now he thinks all the time about the "good old days." He was young then.

【範例 1-2】

　　The old man began to tell us the story of his life, and he started with the year he was fifteen.　He ran away to sea at that age, and he traveled to South America, China, and Australia.　He became too old to work, and came to this country with relatives.　Now he thinks all the time about the "good old days," and he was young then.

【範例 1-3】

　　The old man began to tell us the story of his life. When he was fifteen, he ran away to sea and traveled to South America, China, and Australia.　When he was too old to work, he came to this country with relatives. Now he thinks all the time about the "good old days" when he was young.

　　範例 1-1 皆為「單句」，範例 1-2 皆為「合句」，兩個段落都是不好的結構。範例 1-3 單複句皆使用，為較佳的段落。

【範例 2-1】

　　I will never drive a car again.　I had an accident today. I was driving up Fourth Avenue.　I saw a bright yellow car. It was being driven by a little old lady.　She obviously did not see the stop sign.　I could not stop in time.　She ran into me. Then she called me a "young hoodlum."

【範例 2-2】

I will never drive a car again. I had an accident today when I was driving up Fourth Avenue. I saw a bright yellow car which was being driven by a little old lady. She obviously did not see the stop sign, and I could not stop in time. She ran into me. Then she called me a "young hoodlum."

我永遠不會再開車。我今天在第四大道開車時,發生了一場車禍。我看到一輛黃色的車,是由一位瘦小的老太太駕駛的。她顯然沒有看到停車號誌,而我無法及時煞車。她撞上我,然後叫我「不良少年」。

【範例 3-1】

Being a teacher has long been my goal in life. It is a noble and professional job. It requires great affection, patience, and dedication. It is also a challenging job. The teacher is faced with students of many different aptitudes. I will have a very good experience while teaching. I consider it a good goal.

【範例 3-2】

Being a teacher has long been my goal in life. It is a noble and professional job which requires great affection, patience, and dedication. It is also a challenging job since

UNIT 5

the teacher is faced with students of many different
aptitudes. I am sure that I will have a very good experience
while teaching and I consider it a good goal.

　　長久以來，當老師一直是我的人生目標。老師是種旣崇高又
專業的工作，必須有極大的愛心、耐心，以及犧牲奉獻的精神。
老師必須面對許多不同程度的學生，所以是具有挑戰性的工作。
我相信在教學期間，一定能獲得很好的經驗，因此我認爲當老師
是個很好的目標。

2. 試用不同的結構修改以下文章。

【例 1】

　　KTV is very popular in Taiwan. It is especially
popular with city residents. Many people are under the
pressure of city life, and they love to sing in a KTV.
They can relax and release their tension. A KTV has
low lighting and loud music, and people easily forget
their shyness and frustrations.

UNIT 5

_____

_____

_____

_____

_____

【例 2】

The house was beautiful. A long sidewalk led up to the door, and rows of flowers stood on either side of the steps. The front of the house was red brick, and the woodwork was painted white.

_____

_____

_____

_____

【例 3】

My hometown is in the beautiful county of Ilan. It is in northeastern Taiwan. Ilan is surrounded by mountains. It has little traffic. It has not been spoiled by swarms of visitors. Ilan is clean and quiet. It claims to have the purest water on the island. Its rivers are less polluted. It is a place of scenic beauty with green fields, mountains and rivers.

_____

_____

_____

_____

UNIT 5

【例 4】

There are many sports and swimming is my favorite of all. *Firstly*, it is beneficial to my health, can make me stronger and more energetic, and also helps to keep me slim. *Besides*, it's a good feeling to jump into the cool water when it is a hot summer day.

_____

_____

_____

_____

【例 5】

It is often said that health is wealth, and this suggests that we should aim for health. In the same way, many people aim for wealth. *In fact*, the goal of good health is much easier to achieve. But the goal of wealth is hard to achieve since if we start trying to be healthy, the results are immediate and concrete and money, *meanwhile*, can take a long time to accumulate.

_____

_____

_____

_____

UNIT 5

3. 歷屆試題觀摩：

【例1】

    For coin collectors who invest money in coins, the value of a coin is determined by various factors.

    _____, scarcity is a major determinant. The rarer a coin is, the more it is worth. Note, _____, that rarity has little to do with the age of a coin. Many thousand-year-old coins often sell for no more than a few dollars because there are a lot of them around, _____ a 1913 Liberty Head Nickel may sell for over one million US dollars because there are only five in existence. _____, the demand for a particular coin will also greatly influence coin values. Some coins may command higher prices because they are more popular with collectors. _____, a 1798 dime is much rarer than a 1916 dime, but the latter sells for significantly more, simply because many more people collect early 20th century dimes than dimes from the 1700s. (102年學測)

(A) *Furthermore*   (B) *however*

(C) *First*   (D) while

(E) *For example*   (F) *Eventually*

【例 2】

Why are diamonds more precious than water? The answer has to do with supply and demand. Being a rare natural resource, diamonds are limited in supply. _____, their demand is high because many people buy them to tell the world that they have money, something which is termed as conspicuous consumption in economics. _____, the scarcity of goods is what causes humans to attribute value. If we were surrounded by an unending abundance of diamonds, we probably wouldn't value them very much. _____, diamonds carry a higher monetary value than water, even though we can find more use for water.

（100 年學測）

(A) *Hence*

(B) *In a sense*

(C) *For example*

(D) *However*

(E) *In other words*

(F) *Eventually*

【例 3】

The sun is an extraordinarily powerful source of energy. _____, the Earth receives 20,000 times more energy from the sun than we currently use. If we used more of this source of heat and light, it could supply all the power needed throughout the world.

We can harness energy from the sun, or solar energy, in many ways. _____, many satellites in space are equipped with large panels whose solar cells transform sunlight directly into electric power. These panels are covered with glass and are painted black inside to absorb as much heat as possible.

Solar energy has a lot to offer. *To begin with*, it is a clean fuel. _____, fossil fuels, such as oil or coal, release harmful substances into the air when they are burned. _____, fossil fuels will run out, but solar energy will continue to reach the Earth long after the last coal has been mined and the last oil well has run dry. (99年指考)

(A) *What's more*   (B) *For instance*

(C) *To make matters worse*   (D) *In contrast*

(E) *After all*   (F) *By the way*

(G) *In fact*   (H) *In a sense*

【例 4】

Fans of professional baseball and football argue continually over which is America's favorite sport. Though the figures on attendance for each vary with every new season, certain arguments remain the same.

_____, football is a quicker, more physical sport, and football fans enjoy the emotional involvement they feel while watching. Baseball, _____, seems more mental, like chess, and attracts those fans that prefer a quieter, more complicated game. _____, professional football teams usually play no more than fourteen games a year. Baseball teams, however, play almost every day for six months. _____, football fans seem to love the half-time activities, the marching bands, and the pretty cheerleaders. _____, baseball fans are more content to concentrate on the game's finer details and spend the breaks between innings filling out their own private scorecards. (95 年學測)

(A) *on the other hand*　　　(B) *To begin with*

(C) *in this way*　　　(D) *Finally*

(E) *In addition*　　　(F) *namely*

(G) *therefore*　　　(H) *On the contrary*

【例 5 】

There are six international science Olympiads in the world. They are all organized with a simple intention— to promote global understanding and mutual appreciation among young scientists in all countries. Each of the six science Olympiads has its specific aims. The aims of the International Mathematical Olympiad (IMO),_____, are three-fold. With arduous but interesting math problems, the _____ aim of the IMO is to discover, to encourage and, _____, to challenge mathematically gifted young people all over the world.

_____, the IMO aims to encourage and establish international exchanges, and participation in any IMO contest fosters friendly relations among young mathematicians. Any IMO contest brings not only young mathematicians together but also their instructors; _____, the IMO has as its _____ aim to create opportunities for the exchange of information on math teaching schedules and practices throughout the world. (91 年指考)

(A) *Secondly*　　　　　　(B) *for example*

(C) *likewise*　　　　　　(D) *in contrast*

(E) *first*　　　　　　　　(F) *most important of all*

(G) *therefore*　　　　　　(H) final

UNIT 6　如何寫結尾句 ✏

I. 結尾句爲總結段落主旨的句子，放在段落的最後。可使用之前學過的表示**結論或摘要的轉承語**引導結尾句。

【範例 ①】

〔主題句〕*Keeping an English diary had many other advantages*. 〔推展句①〕*For one thing*, I could train myself to write an exceptional essay by practicing every day. 〔推展句②〕*In addition*, the diary helped me record some happy memories. It was like a friend with whom I could share my feelings or secrets. 〔推展句③〕*Most important of all*, my parents couldn't read my diary because they hadn't learned English. Whatever I wrote, they wouldn't understand. 〔結尾句〕*In short*, *keeping an English diary was a wonderful thing in my life*.

　　寫英文日記也有許多其他的優點。首先，藉由每天練習，我可以訓練自己寫出很棒的文章。此外，這本日記也幫我記錄了一些愉快的回憶。它就像是個朋友，我可以和它分享我的感覺或秘密。最重要的是，爸媽不會看我的日記，因爲他們沒學過英文。無論我寫什麼，他們都看不懂。總之，寫英文日記在我的生活中是一件很棒的事。

【範例②】

　　〔主題句〕*I have good reasons for staying in Taiwan to study*. 〔推展句①〕*First of all*, studying abroad is very expensive. It would be a great burden for me and my family to take on this expense. 〔推展句②〕*Second*, I would prefer to study my core subjects in my own language. I want to be sure that I completely understand the key concepts. While some people say that it is necessary to go abroad in order to gain international experience, I don't agree. People of the world today are closely connected through technology. 〔推展句③〕*In addition*, Taiwan receives visitors from many different countries. *Therefore*, I can learn about other cultures right here if I make the effort. 〔結尾句〕*In conclusion*, *for me*, *Taiwan offers a good education and good opportunities*.

　　我有很好的原因留在台灣唸書。首先,出國讀書非常昂貴。要承擔這項費用對我和我的家人而言,都是一大負擔。第二,我比較想要用我自己的母語研讀我的主科。我要確定我完全理解最重要的概念。雖然有些人說,要獲到國際經驗就必須出國,我不太同意。現在,全世界的人都透過科技緊密地結合在一起。此外,台灣有來自許多不同國家的訪客。因此,只要我努力,在本地也可以很了解其他的文化。總之,對我而言,台灣就提供了良好的教育和好的機會。

UNIT 6

Ⅱ. 主旨句和結尾句各為段落的開頭和結尾，所以可以把握主旨句的關鍵字來寫結尾句，以便頭尾呼應。

【範例 ①】

〔主題句〕Unlike most students, *I don't care for summer*. 〔推展句①〕*For one thing*, although I enjoy being free of school and the responsibility of doing homework every day, I sometimes miss the sense of purpose that school gives me. I find that when I have too much free time, I tend to waste it. 〔推展句②〕*Besides that*, I miss my friends from school. Many of them live too far away, so I cannot see them outside of school. Others are busy with their families or go on a summer trip. *Therefore*, I sometimes feel bored in summer. 〔推展句③〕*Another* reason that I dislike summer is the weather. It is simply too hot. I enjoy outdoor activities, but I don't like to sweat too much. *Because of this*, I am less likely to play sports or even go for a walk during the hot months. 〔結尾句〕*For all of these reasons*, *I am usually happy to see the end of summer*. I enjoy having a break from school, but the summer is too long and too hot for me.

　　和大多數人不同的是，我並不喜歡夏天。首先，雖然我喜歡不用上學、免除每天寫作業的責任，但我偶爾會想念上學給我的那份目的感。我發現當我空閒時間太多時，我很容易就會浪費掉。除此之外,我想念學校裡的朋友。他們許多人都住得太遠了,所以我在校外無法見到他們。還有些人會忙著和家人相處,或是去度暑假。因此,我在夏天有時會感到很無聊。另外一個我不喜歡夏天的原因是天氣,實在是太熱了。我喜歡戶外活動,但我不喜歡流太多汗。因此,我在炎熱的月份裡,比較不可能去從事運動,或甚至去散步。因為所有這些原因,我通常會很高興看到夏天結束。我喜歡放假,但夏天對我而言,太過漫長,也太炎熱。

【範例 ②】

〔主題句〕**My pocket watch is significant** for several reasons. 〔推展句①〕*First of all*, it was my grandfather's, and he used it throughout his life. I can remember him looking at it, touching it and polishing it. My amazing grandfather and the pocket watch are connected in my memory. 〔推展句②〕*Secondly*, I received this watch for my birthday. I was so surprised when I opened the small box from my father and saw the watch. I realized that my father trusted me with this precious object, and this made me feel great. 〔推展句③〕*Finally*, the watch represents time itself. Time can go too fast and we must use it wisely and enjoy life. 〔結尾句〕*After all*, life is short, and my grandfather's *watch reminds me that time is a precious resource*.

　　我的懷錶意義重大，有幾個原因。首先，那是我祖父的，而且他用了一輩子。我還記得他看這只懷錶、撫摸並擦拭它的樣子。我了不起的祖父和這只懷錶，在我的記憶裡是連結在一起的。第二，我在生日時收到這隻錶當禮物。當我打開父親送的小盒子，看到這只錶時，我太驚訝了。我知道父親將這個珍貴的物品託付給我，這讓我覺得很棒。最後，這只錶也象徵了時間本身。時光流逝太快了，我們應該明智地利用，並且好好享受人生。畢竟，我祖父的一生太短暫了，而他的錶提醒了我，時間是一項非常珍貴的資源。

Ⅲ. 請閱讀以下文章，儘可能使用**轉承語**，寫一句結尾句。

【例 1】

　　The Romans organized their empire well. Wherever they ruled, the Romans made Latin a common language. They brought Roman law and Roman citizenship. They took native men into the Roman army. Key cities and highways were built to consolidate their power.

　　〔結尾句〕_____.

【例 2】

　　During the Middle Ages, classes at the University of Paris began at 5 a.m. All morning, students attended their regular class lectures, and all afternoon they attended special lectures. After twelve hours of classes, the students had sports events. Then came homework—copying, recopying, and memorizing notes.

　　〔結尾句〕_____.

UNIT 6

【例 3】

　　Twenty years ago, the southern states of the U.S. began attracting essential industries. The impact of the industrial activity was felt by vast numbers of the populace. For the majority, the change meant higher incomes, improved living standards, better schools, and a richer cultural life than they had known before.

〔結尾句〕 _____.

【例 4】

　　In my opinion, students can learn more and learn more quickly with the help of modern technology. The piece of technology most important as a learning tool must be the computer. Paired with the Internet, it allows students to research topics more quickly and thoroughly and to write up their findings more rapidly as well. *Furthermore*, advances in many fields are being made so fast these days that it is impossible for textbooks to keep up. Technology allows students to keep abreast of the latest developments. *Also, it cannot be denied that* many students enjoy using such resources in their studies. *Because of this*, they are more likely to pursue subjects in greater depth.

〔結尾句〕 _____.

【例5】

　　We should never give up. ***One reason is that*** if we give up too easily, we will rarely achieve anything. It is not unusual for us to fail in our first attempt at something new, so we should not feel discouraged and should try again. ***Besides***, if we always give up when we fail, we will not be able to develop new skills and grow as people. ***Another reason*** we should never give up is that we can learn from our mistakes only if we make a new effort. If we do not try again, the lesson we have learned is wasted. ***Finally***, we should never give up because as we work to reach our goals, we develop confidence, and this confidence can help us succeed in other areas of our lives. If we never challenge ourselves, we will begin to doubt our abilities.

　〔結尾句〕 _____ .

【例6】

　　There are several reasons why I prefer traveling with someone else. ***For one thing***, when I travel with a companion, I have someone with whom to share what I experience. We can talk over the day's events and discoveries, and this will make them more interesting. ***In addition***, it is often comforting to have a familiar person around when we are in a strange environment. When I am traveling in a foreign country, I may be unable to speak the language or may be confused by the local customs. With a travel companion, I will always have someone to talk and share my feelings with. *Finally*, a travel companion can make the journey easier and safer. We can help each other to take care of our bags and get information, as well as keep each other company while waiting in long lines.

〔結尾句〕_____.

【例 7】

Living life at a slower pace has many advantages. *First of all*, slowing down allows us to think more clearly about what we must do. With careful consideration we will make better decisions and make fewer mistakes. *Furthermore*, when we do not have to correct the mistakes that we make in haste, we will actually save time. *Second*, when we take our time, we can do things more carefully and thoroughly. When we do a better job, we will feel more satisfied with our efforts. *Finally*, if we do not rush through life, we will have more time to enjoy the things that we do, and when we take pleasure in our work, we will live happier lives.

〔結尾句〕 _____.

【例 8】

　　To me, a reliable friend is more valuable than one that is intelligent or has a great sense of humor. There are several reasons for my preference. *First of all*, a reliable friend will always stand by me. He may not always know the answer, but he will always have time for my question. He may not get the latest jokes, but neither will he make a joke out of me. *Second*, such a friend will never let me down. I know he will keep his promises and will never reveal my secrets. *Finally*, a reliable friend will be a friend forever. No matter where our lives may take us in the future, I know he will not forget me.

〔結尾句〕 _____.

【例 9】

　　In my opinion, self-employment offers many advantages that owning a business and being an employee do not. *For one thing*, it would allow me to make my own decisions. While a business owner also makes decisions, he is constrained by his responsibilities to his employees. *For another*, the rewards are greater for those who are self-employed than for those who work for others. Granted there is more risk involved, but it would also be satisfying to know that any success was due to my own effort and was mine alone. *Finally*, self-employment is more flexible. I would be able to set my own hours and turn down any job I did not wish to do.

〔結尾句〕_____.

【例 10】

　　Historic buildings are a valuable part of our heritage. *For one thing*, they are a symbol of the past. They remind us of where we came from. *For another*, they may have historical significance. Some important events took place in some of these buildings. If they were lost, we might forget these events as well. *Still another*, they are unique. Buildings like these are not built nowadays because it would be too expensive. *Finally*, they are beautiful. Preserving them would make our city more attractive.

　　〔結尾句〕_____.

UNIT 7 如何寫文章

I. 文章的形成

文章和段落的構造非常相似,段落其實就是迷你短文,將段落組織放大,就成了一篇文章。把主題句擴大變成引言段;推展句擴大成推展段;結尾句擴大成結論段。

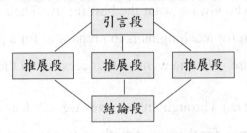

【範例 ①】

Parents Are the Best Teachers

〔引言段〕We will all have many teachers in our lives. They include not only our teachers in school, but our classmates and friends, our colleagues and our bosses and, most importantly, our parents. ***Our parents are our first and best teachers*** because they teach us the most important things in life, teach us continually and always have our best interests at heart.

〔推展段〕*First*, our parents begin teaching us the moment we are born, and what they teach us in those early years are the most important things we can learn. They teach us what is important in our own culture and how to get along with other people. *In addition*, they teach us how to be independent and how to learn. *Of course*, they also teach us language and many other practical skills. *Second*, our parents are always teaching us whether we realize it or not. They teach us both in words and by example. *Finally*, our parents are devoted teachers who always want the best for us. Their only motivation for teaching us is to prepare us for a good life in the future. No one wants our success more than they do.

〔結論段〕Throughout our lives we will learn from many people, for there is something that we can learn from everyone we meet. *However*, no teacher can take the place of our parents because *they are our most devoted and best teachers*.

父 母 是 最 好 的 老 師

我們一生當中會有許多老師,其中不只包括學校的老師、同學和朋友、同事與老闆,最重要的是,還有父母。父母是我們最初、也是最好的老師,因為他們教導我們生活中最重要的事情,他們會不斷地教導我們,而且總是非常關心我們的利益。

第一,父母從我們出生的那一刻起,就開始教導我們,而且他們在最初的那幾年所教導的,都是我們必須學習很重要的事情。父母教導我們,在自己的文化中,什麼是重要的,以及如何與人相處。此外,他們也教導我們如何獨立,以及如何學習。當然,他們也教我們語言,以及很多其他實用的技能。第二,不管我們是否有察覺到，父母總是不斷地以言教及身教的方式教導我們。最後，父母是最盡心盡力的老師，總是想給我們最好的。他們教導我們的唯一動機，就是想幫我們為將來的美好生活做準備。沒有人比他們更希望我們成功。

在我們的一生中，我們會向很多人學習，因為在我們所遇到的每個人身上，一定都有可供學習的地方。然而，沒有老師可以取代父母的地位，因為他們是我們最盡心盡力，同時也是最好的老師。

【範例②】

The Advantages of City Life

〔引言段〕There are undeniable advantages to both life in a big city and in a small town. The former offers more excitement and convenience while the latter offers a cleaner, quieter and often friendlier place to live. *However*, despite the advantages of small town life, *I prefer to live in a big city for several reasons*.

〔推展段〕*First*, life in the city is more convenient. More goods are available and stores are open later. *Also*, there is better public transportation, so it is easier to get around. I can find almost anything I want easily in the city. *Second*, there are more ways to spend leisure time in the city. There are many places I can go to meet friends and have fun. *Finally, and most importantly*, the city offers more educational and career opportunities. The city often attracts the best teachers and the best companies. There is also a wider choice of jobs so it is easier to move up the career ladder.

〔結論段〕*For all of these reasons*, *I prefer to live in the city*. Although I sometimes miss the fresh air and quiet life of a small town, nothing can make up for the opportunities that the city offers me. If one wants to be successful, I believe the best place to live is the city.

都市生活的優點

在大都市和在小城鎮生活各有優點,這是不可否認的。前者提供人們比較多的刺激及便利,而後者則提供一個比較乾淨、安靜,而且通常較友善的居住環境。然而,儘管小鎮生活有這些優點,但基於某些理由,我還是比較喜歡住在大都市。

首先,都市生活比較方便,可以買到比較多商品,而且商店營業時間都比較晚。此外,都市裏有較好的大眾運輸工具,要到哪裏都比較容易。在都市裡,我幾乎可以輕易地找到任何我想要的東西。其次,在都市有比較多的方法,可以消磨空閒時間。有很多地方可以讓我去認識朋友,並且玩得很開心。最後一項要點是,都市提供更多教育及就業的機會。都市往往能吸引最好的老師以及最好的公司。因為工作的選擇比較多樣,所以要升遷也比較容易。

基於上述種種理由,我比較喜歡住在都市。雖然有時候我會想念小鎮新鮮的空氣及安靜的生活,但沒有什麼可以彌補都市提供給我的機會。如果想要成功,我認為最好的居住地點就是都市。

II. 文章的引言段

1. 引言段就如同段落的主題句，讓後面的推展段有所遵循，差別
   在於，要把**主題說明得比較詳細**，以讓讀者更了解主題並有清
   楚的線索。因此，一樣要把握兩個原則：

   a. 表明文章的主題，敘述題目的相關背景。

   b. 段落最後用「引言段的結尾句」表明立場，並引導推展段。

【範例 ①】

Jobs I Wouldn't Want to Have

〔引言段〕Senior high school students spend a lot
of time dreaming about their future. Most of us have a
dream job, but we spend little time thinking about the
opposite—the jobs we would hate. 〔結尾句〕*In my case,
the jobs I would never want to have fall into two categories*.

〔推展段 ①〕*The first* is jobs that are unpleasant or
dangerous. *For example*, I would never want to be a
cleaner or a construction worker. I would find it
disgusting to pick up after other people, and I am
terrified of heights.

〔推展段 ②〕*The second* type of job I wouldn't want
is one that is too hard for me because I would feel a lot
of stress every day. *For instance*, I would never want
to be an accountant because I'm not very good at math.
I would live in constant terror of making a mistake. *In*

the end, I think the best job for me is one that matches my abilities and is something that I will enjoy doing.

我不想從事的工作

　　高中生都會花很多時間，夢想自己的未來。我們大多數的人，都會有夢想中的工作，但我們卻很少去想相反的情況——自己會討厭什麼工作。就我而言，我絕不會想要從事的工作，可分成兩類。

　　第一種就是會令人不愉快或危險的工作。例如，我絕不想要當清潔人員或是建築工人。我覺得替別人收拾善後很噁心，而且我有懼高症。

　　第二種我不想要從事的工作，就是對我而言太困難的工作，因為我每天都會覺得壓力很大。例如，我絕不會想要當會計師，因為我對數學不是很精通。我經常會因為害怕犯錯而生活在恐懼中。最後，我認為最適合我的工作，就是能符合我的能力，而且我又很喜歡做的工作。

【範例 ②】

My Plan for the Next Ten Years

　　〔引言段〕It is very important to have dreams, but it is even more important to have a plan for reaching them. My dream is to run my own business, so 〔結尾句〕*I have developed a ten-year plan in order to achieve it*.

　　〔推展段〕*My plan consists of four stages. The first* part is university. During my time there, I will not only study business, but also build up a network of close friends with similar plans.　*Then* I will work at an international firm for two years in order to gain some experience.　I will try to work in as many departments as possible so that I will have a broad perspective.　*After that*, I will go to the U.S. to earn my MBA.　This will enable me to learn more advanced concepts, polish my English, and make more excellent connections.　*Finally*, I will establish my business.　The first couple of years will be tough, but I'm sure that I will be able to handle the problems.

〔結論段〕*This ten-year plan is very important to me*. I don't want to just waste my life; I want to take charge of my future!

我對未來十年的計畫

有夢想是很重要的，但更重要的是，要有實現夢想的計畫。我的夢想是經營自己的事業，所以爲了實現夢想，我已經做了一個十年的計畫。

我的計畫包含四個階段。第一個部份是大學。在我唸大學的期間，我不僅會研讀商科，也會跟志同道合的密友建立人際網路。然後我會在國際公司上班兩年，以獲得一些經驗。我會儘可能在許多部門工作，以拓展眼界。之後，我會前往美國攻讀企管碩士。這會使我學到更多先進的概念、加強我的英文，並建立更好的人際關係。最後，我會建立自己的事業。前幾年將會很困難，不過我確定，我將能應付所有的問題。

這個十年計畫對我而言很重要。我不想浪費生命；我想要掌控自己的未來！

2. 段落與段落之間，必須相互關連，全篇文章才能連貫。以下文章，
   請依照提供的內容，寫出符合上下文的「引言段的結尾句」，引導
   下一段文章的主旨。

【例 1】

Whether High School Students Should
Wear Uniforms

It probably goes without saying that most high school students do not like to wear uniforms. _____ _____.

Despite these common complaints, I think uniforms are needed for two reasons. *First*, the uniforms let people know who is a student and who is not. *Second*, school uniforms help to create a brotherly feeling among the students of the same school.

All told, I think students should continue to wear uniforms. *In my view*, the benefits of uniforms outweigh their disadvantages.

【例 2】

How to Make Friends

No man is an island. *So* knowing how to make friends is an important thing in our lives. Some people say that making friends is difficult. _____ _____.

First of all, you should smile. People do not like to be with people who have a long face all the time, not to mention make friends with them. *So* try to leave a favorable and pleasant impression on people.

Second, you should be sincere. Everyone likes to be friends with those who are sincere because no one likes the possibility of being deceived by others.

Third, you should help people. A proverb says, "A friend in need is a friend indeed." It obviously shows that friends must support each other and that helping each other will make the friendship even stronger.

As long as you are friendly, honest, and dependable, making friends should be a wonderful experience for everyone involved.

【例 3 】

How to Improve Your English

English is now the international language and so it is very important to learn English well. _____

_____.

There are three ways in which we can improve our English. *First of all*, we have to learn many English words and study English grammar in great detail. *Secondly*, besides learning to read English, we must learn to understand spoken English and practice speaking and writing. *Thirdly*, we should try to talk with English speakers.

There is no shortcut to learning English. If we are prepared to work hard at it, we will be successful in the end.

Ⅲ. 文章的結論段

1. 結論段就如同段落的結尾句，總結全文，使整篇文章有頭有尾，
留給讀者完整的概念或訊息。因此，要把握兩個原則：

a. 總結全文，頭尾呼應，把握「關鍵字」，不可有新的訊息。
b. 使用表示總結的轉承語。

【範例 ①】

Judging a Person by His Appearance

〔引言段〕We all meet a variety of people every day.
When we meet someone new, we soon form an opinion of
that person. Many factors may influence our judgment,
including the person's physical appearance, dress, speech,
body language, and so on. Some people say that it is
unfair to judge a person according to his appearance, for
things such as character and ability are more important.
*No doubt this is true, but I cannot agree with the statement
that one should never judge a person by his external
appearance* because it is a factor we cannot ignore.

〔推展段〕The way a person dresses can be an
important clue because people use such things as dress,
hairstyle, and so on to express themselves. Observing a
person's appearance can often tell us a lot about him or
her. It can tell us if the person identifies with a certain
group and, *more importantly*, how he sees himself.

In addition, we should notice whether a person has dressed appropriately for the occasion. If not, we know that he either does not respect the occasion or is careless. These can also be important clues to his character. *Finally*, although it is wrong to judge people according to stereotypes, we cannot ignore the fact that they are sometimes true. *In other words*, if a person looks dangerous, he might really be a threat, so we should be careful until we know him better.

〔結論段〕*In conclusion*, *I believe that we cannot ignore the importance of external appearance when forming first impressions of someone*. It may not be the most important factor, but it can tell us a lot about the person's character. *Therefore*, we should not only notice others' appearances, but our own as well.

以貌取人

　　我們每天都會遇到各式各樣的人,當我們剛認識某人,就會馬上評斷這個人。影響我們判斷的因素很多,包括這個人的外貌、穿著、談吐、肢體語言等。有人說,根據外表來評斷某人是不公平的,因為像是性格、能力等特質更為重要。無疑地,這樣的說法沒錯,但是我不同意絕對不能以貌取人的說法,因為外表是我們無法忽略的因素。

　　一個人的穿著打扮可能是重要的線索,因為人們會利用像是服裝、髮型等特色,來表達自我。觀察一個人的外表,往往可以讓我們知道很多關於這個人的事情。我們可以知道這個人是不是認同某個團體,而且更重要的是,這個人對自己有何看法。此外,我們應該注意這個人的穿著，在當時的場合是否恰當。如果不恰當，我們就可以知道，這個人並不尊重這個場合，或者是很粗心。這些都可能是觀察其個性的重要線索。最後，雖然根據刻板印象來判斷一個人是錯誤的，但有時我們也不能忽視有時事正確的。換句話說，如果某人看起來很危險，他可能真的是個危險份子，所以在我們更了解他的為人之前，應該要小心謹慎。

總之，我認為當我們對某人形成第一印象時，不能忽略外表的重要性。外表可能並非是最重要的因素，但我們可以從一個人的外表，得知許多與其個性有關的事情。因此，我們不只要注意別人的外表，也要注意自己的外表。

【範例 ②】

Self-Employment

〔引言段〕There are many types of careers from which we can choose. It is most important to choose work that is fulfilling for us, but it is also important to consider our preferred working style. Given the choice between working for someone else, owning a business or being self-employed, I would choose the last one.

〔推展段〕*In my opinion, self-employment offers many advantages that the other two do not. For one thing*, it would allow me to make my own decisions. While a business owner also makes decisions, he is constrained by his responsibilities to his employees. *For another*, the rewards are greater for those who are self-employed than for those who work for others. Granted, there is more risk

UNIT 7

involved, but it would also be satisfying to know that any success was due to my own effort and was mine alone. *Finally*, self-employment is more flexible. I would be able to set my own hours and turn down any job I did not wish to do.

〔結論段〕*In short*, ***self-employment offers more freedom*** than either owning a business or working for someone else, and that is why I would prefer it. *However*, these advantages do not come without cost, for while my success would belong solely to me, so would my failures. *Therefore*, being self-employed requires both courage and competence.

自由業

有很多種職業供我們選擇。選擇有成就感的工作固然重要,但考慮到個人偏好的工作方式也很重要。如果要從受僱於他人、自己創業,或做自由業中做選擇,我會選擇最後一個。

在我看來,自由業提供許多其他兩者沒有的好處。首先,做自由業可以自己做決定。雖然創業者也可以自己做決定,但他對員工有責任,因此會受到限制。其次,做自由業的報酬,也比受僱於他人高。就算風險會比較大,但知道成功是歸因於自己的努力,而且屬於自己一人,會讓人很滿足。最後,做自由業較有彈性。我可以訂定自己的上班時間,也可以拒絕任何不想做的工作。

簡言之,自由業比創業或受僱於他人更自由,這就是我比較喜歡自由業的原因。然而,享有這些好處是要付出代價的,因為成功固然完全屬於我,但失敗也是要自己承擔。因此,做自由業需要具備勇氣及能力。

2. 以下文章，請依照提供的內容，寫出符合上下文的結論段：

【例1】

Maintaining a Habit of Reading

In our modern society, it is necessary for us to constantly learn new knowledge to keep up with the technological advances in science. *The best way of doing this* is to maintain a regular habit of reading.

By reading a scientific magazine, we can remain up-to-date with all the latest scientific inventions. If we regularly read magazines written in English, it will be easier for us to remember the many new words we come across.

_____

_____.

_____.

【例2】

To Learn from Failure

Whenever we do anything, we should keep in mind that "failure is the mother of success." *In other words*, if we learn from our failures, we can still succeed in everything we try to do.

As high school students, we often get discouraged by failure while preparing for the college entrance exam.

But those of us who can learn from these mistakes or failures will probably stand a better chance of getting into a college.

_____

_____.

So, if at first you do not succeed, try, try, try again!

【例 3 】

Movie Theaters or Home Viewing

As a rule, moviegoers have several choices to make. *Besides* having a wide variety of films to choose from, we also have to decide where to watch a movie—at home or in a cinema. Unless it is a new release, such as *Les Misérables*, or a particularly special film like *Transformers* in 3-D, I prefer to watch movies on DVD in the comfort of my home.

Watching a film at home has many advantages. *First of all*, it is usually cheaper than going to a movie theater. For the price of one DVD rental, my whole family or a group of friends can enjoy a film. *Moreover*, we can watch it at our own pace. *Another* reason I like watching movies at home is that I am free to express my feelings. *Thus*, I can laugh or cry as loud as I want without attracting unwanted attention, and *as a result*, have a more enjoyable viewing experience. *Finally*, I can eat whatever I want. My options are not limited to overpriced popcorn and soda.

_____

_____.

That is why I prefer to rent DVDs.

【例 4】

What the World Would Be Without Oil

As we all know, oil is becoming more and more important in the modern society in which we live. *In fact*, oil appears to have become the life-blood of industry.

Without oil, cars, buses and all other forms of transport would no longer be able to move. All the machines in the factories would grind to a halt. *Besides* being unable to travel, workers would have no jobs. Social problems would rapidly increase. The electricity we use could no longer be produced and so we would live in the dark.

_____

_____.

Our lives would be miserable indeed.

【例 5】

Life Is an Experience

As each day passes by, we gain more experience. Those who have lived longest and have done the most things have gained the most experience.

In life, sometimes we are successful and sometimes we fail. When we make mistakes, we should not become discouraged but *instead* learn from our experiences. A proverb says, "Failure is the mother of success." We will succeed in the end if we do not give up.

_____

_____.

By learning from our experiences we can live more comfortable lives.

3. 歷屆試題觀摩：

【例 1】

In English-speaking cultures, the choice of first names for children can be prompted by many factors: tradition, religion, nature, culture, and fashion, to name just a few.

_____ *Some* families have a tradition of passing down the father's first name to the first born son. *In other families*, a surname is included in the selection of a child's given name to keep a family surname going. _____

UNIT 7

_____ Boys' names such as John, Peter, and Thomas are chosen from the Bible. Girls' names such as Faith, Patience, and Sophie (wisdom) are chosen because they symbolize Christian qualities. *However*, for people who are not necessarily religious but are fond of nature, names involving things of beauty are often favored. Flower and plant names like Heather, Rosemary, and Iris fall into this category.

_____ People may choose a name because they are strongly drawn to a character in a book or a television series; they may *also* adopt names of famous people or their favorite actors and actresses. *Sometimes*, people pick foreign names for their *children* because those names are unusual and will thus make their children more unique and distinctive.

_____ *However*, even these people may look at the calendar to pick a lucky day when they make their choice.
（103 年學測）

(A) It may be the mother's maiden name, *for instance*.

(B) *Finally*, some people just pick a name the sound of which they like, regardless of its meaning, its origins, or its popularity.

(C) Certain people like to give a name that has been handed down in the family to show respect for or to remember a relative whom they love or admire.

(D) *For a long time*, religion has also played an important role in naming children.

(E) *Another* factor that has had a great impact on the choice of names is the spread of culture through the media.

【例 2】

　　Many people like to drink bottled water because they feel that tap water may not be safe, but is bottled water really any better?

　　_____ Processing the plastic can lead to the release of harmful chemical substances contained in the bottles into the water. The chemicals can be absorbed into the body and cause physical discomfort, such as stomach cramps and diarrhea. _____ Bacteria can multiply if the water is kept on the shelves for too long or if it is exposed to heat or direct sunlight. Since the information on storage and shipment is not always readily available to consumers, bottled water may not be a better alternative to tap water.

　　_____ It contributes to global warming. An estimated 2.5 million tons of carbon dioxide were generated in 2006 by the production of plastic for bottled water.

　　_____ According to one research study, 90% of the bottles used are not recycled and lie for ages in landfills.

（99年學測）

(A) ***Besides these safety issues***, bottled water has other disadvantages.

(B) Bottled water is mostly sold in plastic bottles and that is why it is potentially health threatening.

(C) Health risks can also result from inappropriate storage of bottled water.

(D) ***In addition***, bottled water produces an incredible amount of solid waste.

(E) ***Needless to day***, disinfecting water is an arduous process.

【例 3】

_____ But it's the parents' job to serve a variety of foods and expose their children to healthy eating habits.

Some simple strategies can help even the pickiest eater learn to like a more varied diet. _____ With hot stoves, boiling water and sharp knives at hand, it is understandable that parents don't want children in the kitchen when they're making dinner. _____ In one study, nearly 600 children from kindergarten to sixth grade took part in a nutrition curriculum intended to get them to eat more vegetables and whole grains. The researchers found that children who had cooked their own foods were more likely to eat those foods in the cafeteria than children who had not. _____

UNIT 7

_____ Kids are tuned into their parents' eating preferences and are far more likely to try foods if they see their mother or father eating them. Given this powerful effect, parents who are trying to lose weight should be careful of how their dieting habits can influence a child's perceptions about food and healthful eating. In one study of 5-year-old girls and their ideas about dieting, one child noted that dieting involved drinking chocolate milkshakes because her mother was using Slim-Fast drinks. Another child said dieting meant "you fix food but you don't eat it." _____ （98 年學測）

(A) *First of all*, you don't have to send children out of the kitchen.

(B) Kids don't usually like radishes, but if kids cut them up and put them in the salad, they will love the dish.

(C) *Another* strategy is not to diet in front of your children.

(D) *But* studies suggest that involving children in meal preparation is an important first step in getting them to try new foods.

(E) Children normally have a distrust of new foods.

(F) By exposing young children to erratic eating habits, parents may be putting them at risk for eating disorders.

【例 4】

Ice sculpting is a difficult process. _____ Its ideal

material is pure, clean water with high clarity. It should also have the minimum amount of air bubbles. Perfectly clear ice blocks weighing 140 kg and measuring 100 cm 50 cm 25 cm are available from the Clinebell Company in Colorado. Much larger clear blocks are produced in Europe and Canada or harvested from a frozen river in Sweden. _____

_____ The temperature of the environment affects how quickly the piece must be completed to avoid the effects of melting. If the sculpting does not take place in a cold environment, then the sculptor must work quickly to finish his piece. The tools used for sculpting also affect when the task can be accomplished. Some sculptures can be completed in as little as ten minutes if power tools are used. _____ The best ice chisels are made in Japan, a country that, along with China, has a long tradition of magnificent ice sculptures.

_____ When holding a dinner party, some large restaurants or hotels will use an ice sculpture to decorate the table. *For example*, at a wedding banquet it is common to see a pair of ice-sculpted swans that represent the union of the new couple. (97 年學測)

(A) Ice sculptures are used as decorations in some cuisines, especially in Asia.

(B) Ice sculptors also use razor-sharp chisels that are specifically designed for cutting ice.

(C) *Another* difficulty in the process of ice sculpting is time control.

(D) *First*, ice must be carefully selected so that it is suitable for sculpting.

(E) These large ice blocks are used for large ice sculpting events and for building ice hotels.

【例 5】

_____ The Chinese emperor Shen Nung in 2737 B.C. introduced the drink. Chinese writer Lu Yu wrote in A.D. 780 that there were "tens of thousands" of teas. Chinese tea was introduced to Japan in A.D. 800. It was then introduced to Europe in the early 1600s, when trade began between Europe and the Far East. _____ Then in 1834, tea cultivation began in India and spread to Sri Lanka, Thailand, Burma, and other areas of Southeast Asia. Today, Java, South Africa, South America, and areas of the Caucasus also produce tea.

_____ Most international tea trading is in black tea. Black tea preparation consists mainly of picking young leaves and leaf buds on a clear sunny day and letting the leaves dry for about an hour in the sun. *Then*, they are lightly rolled and left in a fermentation room to develop scent and a red color. *Next*, they are heated several more times. _____ Green tea leaves are heated in steam, rolled, and dried. Oolong tea is prepared similarly to black tea, but without the fermentation time.

_____ The Chinese variety, a strong plant that can grow to be 2.75 meters high, can live to be 100 years old and survives cold winters. The Assamese variety can grow 18 meters high and lives about 40 years. The Cambodian tea tree grows five meters tall.

_____ Because so many people continue to drink the many varieties of tea, it will probably continue as the world's most popular drink. (95 年學測)

(A) *Finally*, the leaves are dried in a basket over a charcoal fire.

(B) *At that time*, China was the main supplier of tea to the world.

(C) There are three kinds of tea: black, green, and oolong.

(D) Three main varieties of tea—Chinese, Assamese, and Cambodian—have distinct characteristics.

(E) Tea was the first brewed beverage.

(F) Tea is enjoyed worldwide as a refreshing and stimulating drink.

UNIT 8 歷屆學測作文範例

106年學測作文範例

提示：請仔細觀察以下三幅連環圖片的內容，並想像第四幅圖片可能的
發展，然後寫出一篇涵蓋每張圖片內容且結局完整的故事。

A Trip to the Amusement Park

The Martin family had been planning their trip to the
amusement park for a long time. They were very excited as
they packed up their van to make the long drive. *However*,
once they hit the road, they were greeted by heavy traffic on
the highway. The drive took three times longer than it should
have. *To make matters worse*, arriving at the amusement park,

they found the place was swarming with crowds of people waiting to enter. And more people were arriving by the minute!

Mr. Martin was furious for a couple of reasons, *but* mainly that they hadn't anticipated the crowds and the bad traffic, and left earlier in the morning. *After all*, it was a holiday weekend. *On the other hand*, the Martin kids were simply too excited about the trip to turn back now. Now, the only thing to do would be to wait in line with everybody else. *Fortunately*, the park manager recognized the situation and opened both gates to speed up the entrance process. *In the end*, the Martins gained access to the park and had a wonderful time.

去遊樂園玩

長久以來，馬丁一家人一直計畫要去遊樂園玩。當他們將行李打包好裝上廂型車，準備要長途開車時，覺得非常興奮。不過，當他們一上路，就遇到公路上大量的車潮。這趟車程所花的時間是平常的三倍。更糟的是，到達遊樂園時，他們發現那裡擠滿了人潮，等著要入園。而且每時每刻都湧入更多的人！

馬丁先生非常憤怒，原因有好幾個，不過最主要的是，他們沒預料到會有大批人潮和擁擠的交通而早一點出門。畢竟，這是個連假週末。另一方面，馬丁家的小孩對這趟行程感到非常興奮，不可能現在回去。現在唯一能做的，就是跟其他人一樣排隊。幸好，遊樂園的經理認清了這個情況，所以把兩個大門都打開，加快入場的過程。最後，馬丁一家人進入了樂園，並且玩得很愉快。

---

* amusement (əˋmjuzmənt) *n.* 娛樂　　***amusement park*** 遊樂園
pack up 打包；收拾　　van (væn) *n.* 廂型車
drive (draɪv) *n.* 開車出遊；車程　　***hit the road*** 上路；出發

greet〔grit〕v. 迎接　　***be greeted by*** 遭遇

heavy traffic 擁擠的交通；塞車

highway〔'haɪ,we〕n. 公路　　time〔taɪm〕n. 倍

to make matters worse 更糟的是 (= *what's worse*)

swarm〔swɔrm〕v. 充滿著 < *with* >　　crowd〔kraud〕n. 人群；群眾

by the minute 每時每刻；以每分鐘計算

furious〔'fjurɪəs〕adj. 憤怒的　　***a couple of*** 幾個 (= *several*)

anticipate〔æn'tɪsə,pet〕v. 預料　　***after all*** 畢竟

holiday weekend 連假週末　　***on the other hand*** 另一方面

simply〔'sɪmplɪ〕adv. 真正地；確實　　***turn back*** 往回走

wait in line 排隊　　fortunately〔'fɔrtʃənɪtlɪ〕adv. 幸運地

recognize〔'rɛkəg,naɪz〕v. 認出；認清　　gate〔get〕n. 大門；出入口

speed up 加速　　entrance〔'ɛntrəns〕n. 入場

process〔'prɑsɛs〕n. 過程　　***in the end*** 最後　　gain〔gen〕v. 得到

access〔'æksɛs〕n. 進入　　***gain access to*** 進入

have a wonderful time 玩得很愉快 (= *have fun* = *have a good time*)

✐105年學測作文範例

提示：　你認為家裡生活環境的維持應該是誰的責任？請寫一篇短文說明
　　　　你的看法。文分兩段，第一段說明你對家事該如何分工的看法及
　　　　厘由，第二段舉例說明你家中家事分工的情形，並描述你自己做
　　　　家事的經驗及感想。

Household Chores

　　The sharing of household chores should be based on
each family member's contribution to his or her overall living
condition and situation. ***For instance***, if my father works a
full-time job and a part-time job on the weekends, he shouldn't
be expected to come home and wash the dishes. ***Likewise***, my
mother also has a full-time job, ***so*** her commitment to household

chores is limited to what she feels comfortable with. *At the same time*, anybody in the household who is not making a contribution to the family is much more likely to be responsible for household chores. My family doesn't do a lot of cooking at home, so *fortunately*, washing the dishes is rarely if ever necessary.

In my house, the two main chores—cleaning and laundry—are shared between me and my older brother, mainly because we are students and contribute absolutely nothing to the family. *So* we take turns and maintain a chore schedule that is posted on the refrigerator each morning. Every day, *following our studies*, we have a list of tasks which must be completed before we can go outside, or watch TV, or play video games. We also do the laundry on alternate weekends, usually on Sunday. Neither my brother nor I mind doing these chores, *and in fact*, we have our preferences. My brother hates scrubbing the toilet bowls and I can't stand the noise of the vacuum cleaner, so we have an agreement. *And* we're happy to be contributing something to the family.

家　　事

家事分工應該基於各個家庭成員對整個居住環境，以及情況的貢獻來決定。舉例來說，如果我父親有全職的工作，並且週末有兼職的工作，他就不該被期待要回家洗碗。同樣地，我母親也有一個全職的工作，所以她對家事的奉獻就限於她覺得能輕鬆完成的。同時，家庭裡的任何一個人，如果是沒有貢獻的，就很可能需要負責家事。我們家不太開伙，所以很幸運的，即便要洗碗，也是很少。

　　在我們家，有兩個主要的家事——打掃和洗衣服——這些是由我和我哥哥分擔的，主要是因為我們是學生，對這個家沒有貢獻。所以我們輪流做，並維持家事的計畫表，每個早上張貼在冰箱上面。每天下課後，我們有一張工作清單要完成，才能外出、看電視，或是打電玩。我們也輪流在週末洗衣服，通常是在星期日。我哥哥和我都不會介意做這些家事，而且事實上，我們有我們的偏好。我哥哥討厭刷抽水馬桶，而我無法忍受吸塵器的噪音，所以我們有個協議。而且我們都很高興能為家庭有所貢獻。

UNIT 8

* household ('haʊs,hold) *adj.* 家庭的　*n.* 家庭；全家人
　chores (tʃɔrz) *n. pl.* 雜事　　***household chores*** 家事
　be based on 根據　　overall ('ovɚ,ɔl) *adj.* 全部的；整體的
　living conditions 生活條件　　situation (,sɪtʃu'eʃən) *n.* 情況
　for instance 舉例來說 (= *for example*)
　expect (ɪk'spɛkt) *v.* 期待　　dishes ('dɪʃɪz) *n. pl.* 餐具；碗盤
　likewise ('laɪk,waɪz) *adv.* 同樣地
　commitment (kə'mɪtmənt) *n.* 奉獻；付出
　contribution (,kɑntrə'bjuʃən) *n.* 貢獻　　***be likely to V.*** 可能～
　be responsible for 對…負責　　***do a lot of V-ing*** 做很多的…
　fortunately ('fɔrtʃənɪtlɪ) *adv.* 幸運地；幸虧
　rarely ('rɛrlɪ) *adv.* 罕見地；很少　　***rarely if ever*** 就算有也很少
　laundry ('lɔndrɪ) *n.* 待洗衣物
　contribute (kən'trɪbjut) *v.* 貢獻 < *to* >
　absolutely ('æbsə,lutlɪ) *adv.* 絕對地；完全地
　take turns 輪流　　maintain (men'ten) *v.* 維持
　schedule ('skɛdʒul) *n.* 預定表；計畫　　post (post) *v.* 張貼
　task (tæsk) *n.* 工作；任務　　***do the laundry*** 洗衣服
　alternate ('ɔltɚnɪt) *adj.* 隔一的　　preference ('prɛfərəns) *n.* 偏好
　scrub (skrʌb) *v.* 刷洗　　toilet ('tɔɪlɪt) *n.* 廁所；馬桶
　toilet bowl 抽水馬桶　　stand (stænd) *v.* 忍受
　vacuum ('vækjuəm) *n.* 真空；吸塵器
　vacuum cleaner 吸塵器 (= *vacuum*)
　agreement (ə'grimənt) *n.* 協議

📝104年學測作文範例

提示： 下面兩本書是學校建議的暑假閱讀書籍，請依書名想想看該書的
內容，並思考你會選擇哪一本書閱讀，爲什麼？請在第一段說明
你會選哪一本書及你認爲該書的內容大概會是什麼，第二段提出
你選擇該書的理由。

Summer Reading

For my summer reading, I would choose *Everyone Is Beautiful: Respect Others and Be Yourself* by Caroline Strong. The book is probably about how to be a good citizen by treating others the way you would want to be treated; *that is*, fairly and with compassion. *Also*, it most likely promotes a positive outlook on life, suggesting that by having respect for others, you may ultimately become more comfortable with yourself. *Above all*, the book may suggest that judging other people is both harmful to them and your own sense of well-being.

I chose this book because I am interested in personal communication. There are times in my life when I struggle with frustrations and obstacles that have been created by other people. This *in turn* makes me angry with myself. *Thus*, I think I could improve my interactions with others by fostering the respect the book probably talks about, *and at the same time*, improve my own sense of self-worth.

暑 假 閱 讀

　　對於我暑假的閱讀，我會選擇凱洛琳‧史特隆所著的「人人皆美麗：尊重他人並做自己」。這本書可能是關於如何能當一個好的公民，透過己所不欲，勿施於人來完成；也就是說，帶著公平並有同情心。另外，這很可能是推廣一個對生命樂觀的態度，指出藉由尊重他人，你可能最後將對你自己感到更自在。最重要的是，這本書可能說，批判他人同時是對他們以及對你自己的幸福是有害的。

　　我選擇這本書，是因為我對人際溝通很感興趣。我生命中有好幾次我奮力對抗他人造成的挫折和障礙。這結果是氣死自己。因此，我覺得我可以改善和他人的互動，藉由培養這本書可能談論的尊重，並且同時增進自我的價值感。

---

* citizen〔ˈsɪtəzn̩〕*n.* 公民　　**that is** 也就是說
fairly〔ˈfɛrlɪ〕*adv.* 公平地　　compassion〔kəmˈpæʃən〕*n.* 同情心
promote〔prəˈmot〕*v.* 促進；倡導；鼓勵
positive〔ˈpɑzətɪv〕*adj.* 正面的　　outlook〔ˈaʊt͵lʊk〕*n.* 看法 < on >
suggest〔sə(g)ˈdʒɛst〕*v.* 指出　　ultimately〔ˈʌltəmɪtlɪ〕*adv.* 最後
above all 最重要的是　　judge〔dʒʌdʒ〕*v.* 批評 (= *criticize*)
sense〔sɛns〕*n.* 感覺　　well-being〔ˈwɛlˈbiɪŋ〕*n.* 幸福
personal〔ˈpɝsn̩l〕*adj.* 人的；有關人的
communication〔kə͵mjunəˈkeʃən〕*n.* 溝通

struggle〔'strʌgl̩〕v. 掙扎；搏鬥　　frustration〔frʌs'treʃən〕n. 挫折
obstacle〔'ɑbstəkl̩〕n. 阻礙　　***in turn*** 結果；後來
improve〔ɪm'pruv〕v. 改善　　interaction〔ˌɪntɚ'ækʃən〕n. 互動
foster〔'fɑstɚ〕v. 培養　　***at the same time*** 同時

✎ 103年學測作文範例

提示： 請仔細觀察以下三幅連環圖片的內容，並想像第四幅圖片可能的
發展，寫一篇涵蓋所有連環圖片內容且有完整結局的故事。

Steve's Lucky Day

　　Irene and Steve were walking home from school. They
each had their own iPhone. Irene liked to text and chat with
her friends, while Steve enjoyed listening to music. This
afternoon, they took a shortcut through the park. ***However***, it

wasn't their usual route. As they entered the park, Irene was texting with her friends and not paying attention to the path, which took a sharp turn to the left. *As a result*, blissfully unaware of her surroundings, Irene bumped her head on a tree, *and* dropped her iPhone. Lost in his music, Steve continued walking without noticing what had happened.

Several minutes later, Steve had to cross a busy street. Still listening to music at a dangerously loud level, he didn't look before stepping out into the roadway. An oncoming driver honked his horn and slammed on his brakes. *Otherwise* he would have hit Steve with his car. *However*, unaware of the danger, Steve continued on his merry way. *Of course*, the driver was furious, and began shouting and cursing, but it was to no avail. It must have been Steve's lucky day.

史帝夫的幸運日

艾琳和史帝夫當時正從學校走路回家。他們各有自己的蘋果手機。艾琳喜歡傳簡訊和朋友聊天,而史帝夫喜歡聽音樂。當天下午,他們走捷徑穿過公園。這不是他們平常走的路徑。當他們走進公園,艾琳正在傳簡訊給朋友,並沒有注意看路,這條路往左邊急轉。感到很快樂,艾琳沒有注意到周圍環境,她的頭撞到樹,摔掉了蘋果手機。沈浸在自己的音樂裡,史帝夫繼續走,沒注意到發生了什麼事。

幾分鐘後,史帝夫必須跨過熱鬧的街。他依然聽著危險高音量的音樂,沒有看路就踏出去。一輛駛近的司機按喇叭並緊急煞車。不過史帝夫沒有意識到危險,繼續快樂地走路。當然,那司機很生氣,開始大叫咒罵,但是枉然。那天一定是史帝夫的幸運日。

* text〔tɛkst〕v. 傳簡訊　　chat〔tʃæt〕v. 聊天
shortcut〔'ʃɔrt,kʌt〕n. 捷徑；近路　　route〔rut〕n. 路線
pay attention to 注意　　path〔pæθ〕n. 小道；小徑
sharp〔ʃɑrp〕adj. 急轉的　　***to the left*** 向左
blissfully〔'blɪsfəlɪ〕adv. 幸福地；極快樂地
unaware〔,ʌnə'wɛr〕adj. 不注意的；未察覺的 <*of*>
surroundings〔sə'raundɪŋz〕n. pl. 周遭環境
bump〔bʌmp〕v. 使撞上 <*on* / *against*>　　drop〔drɑp〕v. 掉落
be lost in 沈迷於　　level〔'lɛvḷ〕n. 程度
at a~level 以~程度　　step〔stɛp〕v. 步行；踏出一步
roadway〔'rod,we〕n. 道路
oncoming〔'ɑn,kʌmɪŋ〕adj. 即將到來的；接近的
honk one's ***horn*** 按喇叭（= *sound one's horn*）
slam on one's ***brakes*** 緊急煞車（= *hit the brakes*）
merry〔'mɛrɪ〕adj. 快樂的　　***on*** one's ***way*** 在路上
furious〔'fjurɪəs〕adj. 憤怒的　　curse〔kɜs〕v. 咒罵
to no avail 無效；枉然（= *in vain*）　　***must have + p.p.*** 當時一定…

📝102年學測作文範例

提示： 請仔細觀察以下三幅連環圖片的內容，並想像第四幅圖片可能的
發展，寫出一個涵蓋連環圖片內容並有完整結局的故事。

In the past, George would sit in the Priority Seat while riding the MRT.　Sitting there, he would bury his nose in his smartphone, unaware that he was depriving others more deserving of the seat.　*For instance*, an elderly man once had to stand for 15 minutes because George didn't care enough to give up his seat.

Then one day, George broke his ankle while playing basketball.　His foot was in a cast and he had to walk with a crutch.　*The very next day*, George was on the MRT and couldn't find a seat.　He noticed a young girl about his age sitting in a Priority Seat.　He wondered, "Doesn't she see me standing here with a crutch?"　*Apparently*, she did not. George was just about to say something when the elderly man sitting next to the girl spoke up.

"Excuse me, dear," the man said kindly to the girl, "*but* would you mind giving up your seat for that boy with the crutch?"　The girl quickly stood up, offering her seat to George.　As he sat down, George realized the importance of Priority Seats and learned a valuable lesson about consideration for others.

以前，喬治在搭乘捷運的時候會坐在博愛座上。坐在那，他會埋首於他的智慧型手機，沒有意識到他剝奪了需要該座位的人使用的機會。舉例來說，一位老先生曾經站了十五分鐘，因為喬治不夠貼心去讓位。

UNIT 8

　　有一天，喬治打籃球時跌斷腳踝。他的腳包石膏，而必須靠枴杖走路。就在隔天，喬治搭乘捷運而找不到座位。他注意到有一位年輕且和他年紀相仿的女孩坐在博愛座上。他想著：「她沒看到我拿著枴杖站在這裡嗎？」她顯然沒有注意到。正當喬治要開口說話時，一位坐在女孩旁邊的老先生說話了。

　　「很抱歉，親愛的，」那位先生親切地對女孩說，「不過妳介意把妳的座位讓給拿著枴杖的男孩嗎？」那位女孩很快就站起來，讓座給喬治。當他坐下後，喬治理解到了博愛座的重要性，並學到了珍貴的一課，關於體諒他人。

*priority〔praɪˈɔrətɪ〕*n*. 優先權　　***priority seat*** 博愛座
the MRT 捷運（ = *the Mass Rapid Transit*）
bury〔ˈbɛrɪ〕*v*. 埋　　***bury*** *one's nose in* 埋首於；沈迷於
smartphone〔ˈsmɑrtˌfon〕*n*. 智慧型手機
unaware〔ˌʌnəˈwɛr〕*adj*. 不知道的；未察覺的
deprive〔dɪˈpraɪv〕*v*. 剝奪　　deserving〔dɪˈzɝvɪŋ〕*adj*. 應得的 < *of* >
for instance 舉例來說　　elderly〔ˈɛldəlɪ〕*adj*. 年長的
give up *one's seat* 讓座　　ankle〔ˈæŋkḷ〕*n*. 腳踝
break *one's ankle* 跌斷腳踝　　cast〔kæst〕*n*. 石膏
in a cast 包石膏　　crutch〔krʌtʃ〕*n*. 拐杖
the next day （過去）隔天　　wonder〔ˈwʌndə〕*v*. 猜想
apparently〔əˈpærəntlɪ〕*adv*. 顯然
be (just) about to V. 即將～；正要～　　***speak up*** 大聲說
mind + V-ing 介意～　　offer〔ˈɔfə〕*v*. 提供
realize〔ˈriəˌlaɪz〕*v*. 了解；領悟
valuable〔ˈvæljəbḷ〕*adj*. 有價值的；珍貴的
learn a lesson 學到教訓　　consideration〔kənˌsɪdəˈreʃən〕*n*. 體諒

📝101年學測作文範例

提示：　你最好的朋友最近迷上電玩，因此常常熬夜，疏忽課業，並受到父母的責罵。你（英文名字必須假設為 Jack 或 Jill）打算寫一封信給他/她（英文名字必須假設為 Ken 或 Barbie），適當地給予勸告。

請注意：必須使用上述的 Jack 或 Jill 在信末署名，**不得使用自己的真實中文或英文名字**。

Dear Ken,　　　　　　　　　　　　　　Jan. 18, 2012

　　You know that I always support you, but you've been spending far too much time playing video games—and suffering the consequences as a result. *Of course*, I love video games too, and I understand how easy it is to get wrapped up in them. *However*, when the games begin to have an effect on your education and relationships, something has to give.

　　Moderation is the key to everything and video games are no exception. I'm not saying you should stop playing video games altogether, but I am strongly suggesting you cut back a little, if for no other reason than to keep your parents off your back. You could try my method, which is to set a limit of two hours per day. I think you'll come to realize that life will be much easier when your parents aren't constantly scolding you. *And besides*, you really don't want to mess up your future, do you? *Anyway*, if there's anything I can do to help you, don't hesitate to ask.

　　　　　　　　　　　　　　　Your friend,
　　　　　　　　　　　　　　　Jack

UNIT 8

親愛的肯：

　　你知道我一直是支持你的，不過你花太多時間玩電玩了——而且也因此嚐到後果了。當然，我也愛電玩，而且我了解沈溺其中有多麼容易。然而，當遊戲影響到你的教育和關係時，必須要有所取捨。

　　所有事情重在適度，而電玩也沒有例外。我不是說你應該完全停止打電玩，而是強烈建議你應該稍微減少打電玩的時間，即便只是為了不讓你的父母嘮叨。你應該嘗試我的方法，就是每天設置兩個小時的電玩時間。我想你會慢慢了解到，沒有你父母一直責備你，生活會更舒適。而且，不會想要搞砸你的未來吧，是嗎？無論如何，如果有什麼我可以幫忙你的，不要猶豫來求救。

你的朋友，

傑克

2012 年 1 月 18 日

* support〔sə'port〕*v.* 支持　　***video game*** 電玩
suffer〔'sʌfə〕*v.* 遭受　　consequence〔'kɑnsə,kwɛns〕*n.* 後果
as a result 因此　　***be wrapped up in*** 醉心於；迷戀
have an effect on 對…有影響　　education〔,ɛdʒə'keʃən〕*n.* 教育
relationship〔rɪ'leʃən,ʃɪp〕*n.* 關係
Something has to give. 要有所改變；要有所取捨。
moderation〔,mɑdə'reʃən〕*n.* 適度；節制
key〔ki〕*n.* 關鍵　　***be no exception*** ～也不例外
altogether〔,ɔltə'gɛðə〕*adv.* 完全　　***cut back*** 減少
keep sb. off one's ***back*** 使某人不嘮叨　　method〔'mɛθəd〕*n.* 方法
constantly〔'kɑnstəntlɪ〕*adv.* 不斷地　　scold〔skold〕*v.* 責罵
mess up 搞砸　　hesitate〔'hɛzə,tet〕*v.* 猶豫

✎100年學測作文範例

提示：請仔細觀察以下三幅連環圖片的內容，並想像第四幅圖片可能的
　　　發展，寫出一個涵蓋連環圖片內容並有完整結局的故事。

Costume Party

Bill and Maryanne met at a costume party and it was love at first sight. Bill was especially attracted to Maryanne's beauty. When the party was over, they exchanged phone numbers and parted ways. *However*, Bill couldn't get Maryanne out of his mind. He decided to make a romantic gesture. *Later that evening*, he appeared outside Maryanne's apartment building with his guitar, prepared to sing a song declaring his love. He began to sing and play under a crescent moon. He thought Maryanne would certainly come to her window.

Unfortunately, Bill's serenade did not produce the reaction he was looking for. *Within minutes*, several angry residents came to their windows and shouted at Bill to stop making so much noise. "Get out of here," one woman shouted, "*or* I will call the police!" Bill was terribly embarrassed by his mistake. "I guess Maryanne doesn't live in that building," Bill said to himself. He quickly apologized and left the scene.

The next morning, Maryanne appeared at Bill's door. "I'm so sorry," Maryanne said. "That was my mother who shouted at you. She's very protective of me. I'm not allowed to have visitors after dark." Bill was relieved that his effort hadn't been wasted.

化 妝 舞 會

比爾和瑪麗安妮在化妝舞會遇見，並且一見鍾情。比爾特別被瑪麗安妮的美麗所吸引。當派對結束後，他們交換電話並各自離開。然而，比爾對瑪麗安妮念念不忘。他決定要有個爛漫的示愛。那天晚上稍後，他出現在瑪麗安妮公寓大樓的外面，帶著吉他，準備唱首歌宣愛。他開始在新月下唱歌彈奏。他覺得瑪麗安妮一定會出現在窗邊。

很不幸的，比爾的小夜曲並沒有如他預期產生他要的反應。在幾分鐘內，好幾位生氣的居民來到窗邊對比爾大喊，要他停止噪音。「滾開這裡，」一位女士大喊，「不然我要報警了！」比爾對他犯的錯感到非常尷尬。「我想瑪麗安妮不是住在那棟樓。」比爾對自己說。他很快地道歉並離開現場。

隔天早上，瑪麗安妮出現在比爾的門口。「我很抱歉。」瑪麗安妮說，對你大喊的是我母親。她非常保護我。我不被允許在天黑後有訪客。」比爾感到放心，他的努力沒有白費。

---

* costume〔ˈkɑstum〕*n.* 服裝　　*costume party* 化裝舞會
love at first sight 一見鍾情

especially〔ə'spɛʃəlɪ〕*adv.* 尤其；特別地
be attracted to 被…吸引　　exchange〔ɪks'tʃendʒ〕*v.* 交換
part〔pɑrt〕*v.* 分開　　***part ways*** 分道揚鑣
get sb. out of *one's* ***mind*** 不再想某人；忘記某人
romantic〔ro'mæntɪk〕*adj.* 爛漫的
gesture〔'dʒɛstʃə〕*n.* 表示；動作　　appear〔ə'pɪr〕*v.* 出現
apartment〔ə'pɑrtmənt〕*adj.* 公寓　　declare〔dɪ'klɛr〕*v.* 宣告
crescent〔'krɛsn̩t〕*n.* 新月
unfortunately〔ʌn'fɔrtʃənɪtlɪ〕*adv.* 不幸地
serenade〔ˌsɛrə'ned〕*n.* 小夜曲　　produce〔prə'djus〕*v.* 產生
reaction〔rɪ'ækʃən〕*n.* 作用；反應　　***look for*** 尋找
resident〔'rɛzədənt〕*n.* 居民　　***call the police*** 報警
apologize〔ə'pɑləˌdʒaɪz〕*v.* 道歉　　scene〔sin〕*n.* 場面；現場
protective〔prə'tɛktɪv〕*adj.* 保護的
be protective of 保護（= *protect*）　　***after dark*** 天黑後
relieved〔rɪ'livd〕*adj.* 感到放心的

UNIT 8

📝99年學測作文範例

提示：　請仔細觀察以下三幅連環圖片的內容，並想像第四幅圖片可能的
　　　　發展，寫出一個涵蓋連環圖片內容並有完整結局的故事。

It was a typical morning in Mrs. Chen's noodle shop. Mrs. Chen's son, Steven, sat at the counter doing his homework while a man ate noodles. The man's bag sat on the stool between them. When he finished his breakfast, the man paid and left the shop. *However*, he forgot his bag on the stool.

Accordingly, Mrs. Chen and Steven opened the bag to find some identification. *To their surprise*, the bag was filled with money. "Run along to school, Steven," Mrs. Chen said. "I'll take care of this." *Meanwhile*, the man got to the train station before he realized the bag was missing. He quickly returned to the noodle shop where Mrs. Chen was holding the bag for him.

"I had a feeling you'd be back," Mrs. Chen scolded the man. "Thank you so much," the man replied. He reached into the bag and pulled out a stack of $1,000 NT notes. "Please," the man said, "take this as a reward for your honesty."

那天是陳太太麵攤平常的早上。陳太太的兒子，史蒂芬，坐在櫃台前做功課，而有一位男士在吃麵。男士的包包放在他們之間的凳子上。當男士吃完早餐，他付錢然後離開店家。不過，他忘了他放在凳子的包包。

因此，陳太太和史蒂芬打開包包，發現一些證件。讓他們驚訝的是包包裡面塞滿了錢。「快跑去學校，史蒂芬，」陳太太說。「這個我會處理。」同時，男士到了車站才發現他的包包不見了。他很快回到麵攤，陳太太正提著包包等他。

　　「我有預感你會回來，」陳太太責備男子。「非常感謝妳，」
那先生回答。他伸手進包包，拿出一疊台幣一千元的鈔票。「請拿
走這個作爲妳誠實的獎賞。」男子說

* typical〔'tɪpɪkḷ〕*adj.* 典型的　　noodle〔'nudḷ〕*n.* 麵
counter〔'kaʊntɚ〕*n.* 櫃台　　sit〔sɪt〕*v.* 被放在
stool〔stul〕*n.* 凳子　　identification〔aɪ,dɛntəfə'keʃən〕*n.* 證件
to one's surpise 令某人驚訝的是　　***run along*** 走開
take care of 處理　　meanwhile〔'min,hwaɪl〕*adv.* 同時
get to 到達　　missing〔'mɪsɪŋ〕*adj.* 找不到的；遺失的
scold〔skold〕*v.* 責罵　　***reach into*** 伸入　　***pull out*** 拿出
stack〔stæk〕*n.* 一疊；一堆　　note〔not〕*n.* 鈔票

📝 98年學測作文範例

提示：

請根據右方圖片的場景，
描述整個事件發生的前因
後果。文章請分兩段，第
一段說明之前發生了什麼
事情，並根據圖片內容描
述現在的狀況；第二段請
合理說明接下來可能會發
生什麼事，或者未來該做
些什麼。

The Earthquake

　　I never thought it'd happen to me. We've all seen poor
people lose their homes, *or even worse*, their lives, to
earthquakes. We sympathize with them, *but at the same time*

are glad it didn't happen to us. *Well*, I can't be glad anymore. My house has been torn apart, and I'm lucky to just be alive.

It's not safe here anymore. Debris and aftershocks are still a danger. *Plus*, the refugee camp is way too crowded. *Therefore*, I plan on moving to my parents' for a while. The news says it'll take at least a year to get everything back on track here. I can't wait that long, so I have to start a new life somewhere else. *Hopefully*, a place without earthquakes.

地　震

我從沒想過這會發生在我身上。我們看過窮人失去他們的家園，或者甚至更糟的，喪生於地震中。我們同情他們，但是同時也很慶幸這沒有發生在我們身上。嗯，我再也慶幸不了了。我的房子被摧毀了，而我只是很幸運的還存活下來。

這裡不再安全了。碎石瓦礫和餘震還是很危險。此外，難民營太擁擠了。因此，我計畫搬到我父母親那裡一陣子。新聞說這至少要花一年才能讓這裡的一切回到正軌。我等不了那麼久，所以我覺得要在其他的地方重新開啓新的生活。希望是一個沒有地震的地方。

* sympathize〔'sɪmpə,θaɪz〕v. 同情 < with >
　　at the same time 同時　　tear〔tɛr〕v. 撕開；扯破
　　debris〔də'bri〕n. 殘骸；碎片　　aftershock〔'æftə,ʃɑk〕n. 餘震
　　refugee〔,rɛfjʊ'dʒi〕n. 難民　　***refugee camp*** 難民營
　　crowded〔'kraʊdɪd〕adj. 擁擠的
　　back on track 回到正軌；恢復正常
　　hopefully〔'hopfəlɪ〕adv. 但願

✍97年學測作文範例

提示： 你（英文名字必須假設爲 George 或 Mary）向朋友（英文名字
必須假設爲 Adam 或 Eve）借了一件相當珍貴的物品，但不愼
遺失，一時又買不到替代品。請寫一封信，第一段說明物品遺失
的經過，第二段則表達歉意並提出可能的解決方案。

請注意： 爲避免評分困擾，請使用上述提示的 George 或 Mary 在信末
署名，**不得使用自己眞實的中文或英文姓名**。

An Apology Letter to Eve

February 2, 2008

Dear Eve,

    I'll be honest with you. I lost your digital camera at the concert last night. I promised I'd be extra careful with it, and I was. *However*, there were so many people yesterday. The crowd got out of hand. When I was taking pictures, people kept bumping into me. The camera fell out of my hand, and there wasn't even space to bend down, let alone look for it. I stayed after the concert and searched, but to no avail.

    Please forgive me. You don't know how sorry I am. I know you had precious pictures in there, not to mention the camera itself. I definitely will pay for a new camera. Just give me some time. *And* to compensate for the pictures and memories, let me take you out to wherever you want. *Again*, I'm truly sorry for what happened, and hope that I can make it up to you.

Your friend,
George

UNIT 8

給伊芙的一封道歉信

親愛的伊芙：

　　我老實跟妳說。我昨天晚上在演唱會弄丟了妳的數位相機。我答應我會特別照顧好它，我當時有。但是，昨天有很多人，而且群眾失去控制。當我在照相時，人們一直撞到我。相機從我的手中掉落，而且甚至沒有空間可以讓我彎下腰，更不用說找相機了。我演唱會結束後留下來找，但是徒勞無功。

　　請原諒我。妳不知道我有多麼愧疚。我知道妳有很多珍貴的相片在那裡面，更不用說相機本身。我一定會付錢買一台新相機。只要給我一點時間。而為了賠償裡面的相片和記憶，讓我帶妳出去到任何妳想要的地方。再說一次，對於所發生的事，我真的很抱歉，並且希望我能補償妳。

你的朋友，

喬治

2008 年 2 月 2 日

* **apology** 〔ə'pɑlədʒɪ〕 *n.* 道歉　　**digital** 〔'dɪdʒɪtl̩〕 *adj.* 數位的
  extra 〔'ɛkstrə〕 *adv.* 特別地；格外地
  crowd 〔kraʊd〕 *n.* 群眾；人群　　***get out of hand*** 變得難以控制
  take a picture 拍照　　***bump into*** 撞上　　**space** 〔spes〕 *n.* 空間
  bend down 彎下腰　　***let alone*** 更不用說 (= *not to mention*)
  search 〔sɝtʃ〕 *v.* 搜尋　　**avail** 〔ə'vel〕 *n.* 效用；效力
  to no avail 徒勞無功 (= *in vain*)
  precious 〔'prɛʃəs〕 *adj.* 珍貴的
  definitely 〔'dɛfənɪtlɪ〕 *adv.* 一定
  compensate 〔'kɑmpən͵set〕 *v.* 賠償；彌補
  memory 〔'mɛmərɪ〕 *n.* 回憶　　**again** 〔ə'gɛn〕 *adv.* 而且；再說
  make it up 彌補

96年學測作文範例

提示： 請以下面編號 1 至 4 的四張圖畫內容為藍本，依序寫一篇文章，
描述女孩與貓之間的故事。你也可以發揮想像力，自己選定一個
順序，編寫故事。請注意，故事內容務必涵蓋四張圖意，力求情
節完整、前後發展合理。

(1) (2) (3) (4)

Jane's New Pet

One day, Jane was playing in the park. She was very
happy to find a little cat to play with. When she went home,
she took the cat with her. *However*, she didn't know that all of
the cat's brothers and sisters were following her.

Jane asked her mother if she could keep the cat as a pet.
Her mother was not happy because she thought a pet would
cause a lot of trouble. *But* Jane promised that she would take
care of the cat well. *Finally* her mother agreed.

Unfortunately for Jane, all of the cats moved into her house and made a big mess. They scratched the sofa and broke a lamp. Their muddy feet made the floor dirty. Poor Jane. She will have to clean up the mess or her mother will be very angry.

UNIT 8

珍的新寵物

有一天，珍在公園裡玩耍。她很高興找到一隻小貓咪一起玩。當她回家的時候，她帶著貓咪一起回家。然而，她不知道貓咪的所有兄弟姊妹在跟著她。

珍問她媽媽是否她可以養貓作為寵物。她媽媽很不高興，因為她認為寵物會造成很多問題。但是珍保證她會好好照顧貓咪。最後她媽媽同意了。

對珍來說，很不幸的是所有的貓咪都搬進了她家，並把家裡搞得亂七八糟。牠們抓沙發並打破檯燈。牠們沾滿泥的腳弄髒了地板。可憐的珍。她將必須清理這一片狼籍，否則她媽媽會很生氣。

* pet〔pɛt〕*n.* 寵物　　follow〔'falo〕*v.* 跟隨　　keep〔kip〕*v.* 飼養
cause〔kɔz〕*v.* 造成；引起　　trouble〔'trʌbl̩〕*n.* 麻煩的事
promise〔'pramıs〕*v.* 承諾；答應　　finally〔'faınlı〕*adv.* 最後
agree〔ə'gri〕*v.* 同意　　*take care of* 照顧
unfortunately〔ʌn'fɔrtʃənıtlı〕*adv.* 不幸地；遺憾地
move〔muv〕*v.* 搬家；遷移　　mess〔mɛs〕*n.* 混亂；亂七八糟
scratch〔skrætʃ〕*v.* 抓傷　　break〔brek〕*v.* 打破；弄壞
lamp〔læmp〕*n.* 燈　　muddy〔'mʌdı〕*adj.* 沾滿泥的
floor〔flor〕*n.* 地板　　dirty〔'dɜtı〕*adj.* 髒的
poor〔pur〕*adj.* 可憐的　　*clean up* 把…打掃乾淨；清理
or〔ɔr〕*conj.* 否則　　angry〔'æŋgrı〕*adj.* 生氣的

📝 95年學測作文範例

提示： 根據下列連環圖畫的內容，將圖中女子、小狗與大猩猩（gorilla）
之間所發生的事件作一合理的敘述。

A Romantic Surprise

A young woman is in her kitchen, stir-frying meat and
vegetables. Her obedient dog is sitting patiently behind her,
enjoying the smell, hoping for some! *Suddenly*, there is a
terrifying growling noise! The startled woman turns and
jumps in fright. She drops a plate of food and screams out,
"Oh, my God!" A big hairy gorilla is coming at her.

Strangely, the dog is unafraid and starts eating the food
happily. *Meanwhile*, the ferocious-looking gorilla takes off
his head. *What a surprise*! It was a mask! The person
underneath the costume is her husband. He smiles and offers
her a beautiful bouquet of flowers. He says sweetly, "Happy
April Fool's Day, honey. I love you!" The woman felt
relieved and overwhelmed with joy. What a big gorilla
surprise!

一場浪漫的意外

　　一位年輕的女士在她的廚房裡面，炒肉伴青菜。她的狗很聽話，耐心地坐在她後面，享受那味道，希望可以吃到一點！突然間，有一個可怕的咆哮聲。受驚的女士轉過頭，驚跳了一下。她掉下一盤食物並尖叫，「喔，我的天呀！」一隻毛茸茸的大猩猩正衝向她。

　　很奇怪的是，那隻狗並不害怕，並開始開心地吃食物。同時，那看起來很凶猛的大猩猩拿下牠的頭。真令人驚訝！那是個面具！那衣服底下的人是她丈夫。他微笑並給她一束美麗的花。他甜蜜地說：「愚人節快樂，親愛的。我愛妳！」女士感到放心而高興不已。真是一個大猩猩的驚喜！

* romantic〔roˋmæntɪk〕*adj.* 浪漫的
  stir-fry〔ˋstɝˏfraɪ〕*v.* 炒（菜）　　meat〔mit〕*n.* 肉
  obedient〔əˋbidɪənt〕*adj.* 順從的；聽話的
  patiently〔ˋpeʃəntlɪ〕*adv.* 有耐心地　　smell〔smɛl〕*n.* 氣味；香味
  suddenly〔ˋsʌdn̩lɪ〕*adv.* 突然地
  terrifying〔ˋtɛrəˏfaɪɪŋ〕*adj.* 可怕的
  growling〔ˋgraʊlɪŋ〕*adj.* 咆哮的　　noise〔nɔɪz〕*n.* 聲音
  startled〔ˋstɑrtl̩d〕*adj.* 吃驚的；驚嚇的　　jump〔dʒʌmp〕*v.* 跳
  fright〔fraɪt〕*n.* 驚嚇；恐怖　　drop〔drɑp〕*v.* 使掉落
  plate〔plet〕*n.* 盤子；一盤的份量　　*scream out* 尖聲喊叫說
  hairy〔ˋhɛrɪ〕*adj.* 毛茸茸的　　gorilla〔gəˋrɪlə〕*n.* 大猩猩
  come at 攻擊；衝向　　strangely〔ˋstrendʒlɪ〕*adv.* 奇怪的是
  unafraid〔ʌnəˋfred〕*adj.* 不怕的
  meanwhile〔ˋminˏhwaɪl〕*adv.* 同時；於此時
  ferocious〔fəˋroʃəs〕*adj.* 兇猛的　　*take off* 拿下
  mask〔mæsk〕*n.* 面具　　underneath〔ʌndɚˋniθ〕*prep.* 在…之下
  costume〔ˋkɑstjum〕*n.* 服裝　　offer〔ˋɔfɚ〕*v.* 給予；提供
  bouquet〔buˋke〕*n.* 花束　　sweetly〔ˋswitlɪ〕*adv.* 甜蜜地；親切地
  April Fool's Day 愚人節

✏️ 94年學測作文範例

提示： 請根據以下三張連環圖畫的內容，以 "In the English class last week,…" 開頭，將圖中主角所經歷的事件作一合理的敘述。

In the English class last week, our teacher taught us Lesson 30 "We Are the World." *However*, I became very bored, and started drifting off and daydreaming. *Before I knew it*, I was sound asleep and having the most unusual dream.

I dreamed that I was teaching up in front of the class. I was trying to explain the fundamentals of English grammar, when, *much to my surprise*, all my students fell asleep. They were snoring, breathing loudly and even drooling! *At first*, I was embarrassed and frustrated, but then I started to get very upset. *Therefore*, I yelled "Wake up!" at the top of my lungs to my snoozing students. My scream startled and scared them to death! *Suddenly*, *in fright*, I opened my eyes and realized that my teacher was yelling those exact same words

at me! Wow! What a shocking surprise! I immediately
realized that I had fallen asleep and had dreamed about a
situation that was happening to me at that very moment.

　　上禮拜的英文課，我們老師教我們第三十課「四海一家」。
不過，我覺得很無聊，並開始昏昏欲睡做白日夢。很快，我就沈
睡了，並做了一個很不尋常的夢。

　　我夢到我在全班面前授課。我正嘗試著要解釋英文文法的基
本原理，這時讓我感到意外的是，我的學生都睡著了。他們在打
呼、發出很大的呼吸聲，並甚至在流口水！一開始，我覺得很尷
尬和挫折感，但是後來我覺得非常沮喪。因此，我用力對著正在
打瞌睡的學生大喊「起床！」。我的尖叫聲嚇到了他們，快把他
們嚇死了！突然間，嚇了一跳，我打開眼睛，發現我的老師正對
著我大喊一樣的話！哇！眞是令人震驚！我馬上了解到我剛剛睡
著了，並夢到當時正發生在我身上一樣的情況。

---

* drift〔drɪft〕v. 漂流　　**drift off** 迷迷糊糊地睡去；出神
daydream〔'de,drim〕v. 做白日夢　　**before I know it** 很快地
be sound asleep 睡得很熟　　fundamental〔,fʌndə'mɛntḷ〕n. 原理
grammar〔'græmɚ〕n. 文法
much to one's **surprise** 令某人感到非常驚訝的是
snore〔snor〕v. 打呼　　drool〔drul〕v. 流口水
embarrassed〔ɪm'bærəst〕adj. 覺得尷尬的
frustrated〔'frʌstretɪd〕adj. 受挫的　　upset〔ʌp'sɛt〕adj. 不高興的
yell〔jɛl〕v. 大叫　　**at the top of** one's **lungs** 以最大的音量
snoozing〔'snuzɪŋ〕adj. 打瞌睡的　　scream〔skrim〕n. 尖叫
startle〔'stɑrtḷ〕v. 驚嚇　　scare〔skɛr〕v. 使害怕
scare sb. **to death** 把某人嚇得半死　　fright〔fraɪt〕n. 驚嚇
exact〔ɪg'zækt〕adj. 確切的；恰好的　　wow〔waʊ〕interj. 哇啊
shocking〔'ʃɑkɪŋ〕adj. 可怕的；令人震驚的
very〔'vɛrɪ〕adj. 正是那一個的

93年學測作文範例

提示： 請根據以下三張連環圖畫的內容，以 "One evening,…" 開頭，
寫一篇文章，描述圖中主角所經歷的事件，並提供合理的解釋與
結局。

The Wrong Taxi

One evening Mr. Chang attended a wedding banquet. The food was wonderful and so was the wine. He had a very good time. *Unfortunately* he drank too much. When Mr. Chang left the party he wondered how he could get home. He knew that he should not drive his car. If he drove his car while drunk, he might cause an accident. *Then* he would be in trouble with the police.

Luckily, as Mr. Chang was thinking about what to do, a taxi passed by. He quickly called the taxi and climbed into the car. The driver said he knew where to go and the car started to move. "What a good taxi driver," Mr. Chang thought. He soon fell asleep.

When Mr. Chang woke up it was morning. ***But*** he was not at home. ***To his surprise***, he was at a police station. The taxi he had taken the night before was not a taxi at all. It was a police car! ***And*** the driver was a police officer, who had taken him directly to the police station.

搭錯計程車

　　有一天傍晚，張先生出席了一場婚宴。食物很棒，酒也是。他度過了美好的時光。不幸的是，他喝太多酒了。當張先生離開宴會時，他想他如何能回到家。他知道他不該自己開車。如果他酒駕，他可能會造成意外。那麼他會招惹警方，受到懲罰。

　　很幸運的，當張先生正在想要怎麼辦，一台計程車開過。他很快叫了計程車並爬進車內。司機說他知道要去哪，車子就開始動了。「真棒的計程車司機呀，」張先生說。他很快就睡著了。

　　當張先生起床時，已經是早上了。但是他不在家裡面。讓他驚訝的是，他在警局裡。昨晚他所搭的其實不是計程車。是警車！而且司機是警察，直接把他載到警察局。

* wedding (ˈwɛdɪŋ) *n.* 結婚典禮
banquet (ˈbæŋkwɪt, ˈbæŋkwɪt) *n.* 宴會
wedding banquet 結婚喜宴
unfortunately (ʌnˈfɔrtʃənɪtlɪ) *adv.* 不幸地
be in trouble with 被…責罵；處罰　　***pass by*** 經過
climb (klaɪm) *v.* 登上（交通工具）
directly (dəˈrɛktlɪ) *adv.* 直接地　　***police station*** 警察局

✏️92年學測作文範例②

提示：請以自己的經驗爲例，敘述當你感到不快樂或情緒低落時，（除了簡答題選文中所提及的方法外，）你最常用哪一種方法幫自己渡過低潮，並舉實例說明這個方法何以有效。

We must all go through hard times in life. We may fail a test, lose our job or simply get caught in an annoying traffic jam. All of these things can make us feel sad or upset. In times such as these it is important to calm down and recover our good spirits. The following is the way I improve my mood when I feel down.

First of all, I tell myself that no matter what happens, it is not the end of the world. Life will go on, and I will overcome the difficulty eventually. *Then* I look for a way to solve my problem. If I can find one, I take action right away. If not, I forget about it for a while. I have found that by putting my troubles and sorrows aside I can have more energy to face challenges. *Therefore*, I will take a break. I will listen to music, watch TV or talk to a friend. *Then*, when I am in a better mood, I can face my problems and solve them.

In short, the best way for me to cheer myself up is to forget my problems for a while. That way I can relax and think clearly. *Then* I can find the best solution. Once I have dealt with the problem I will be able to smile again.

UNIT 8

　　我們一定都會經歷生命中艱苦的時候。我們可能會考試不及格，失業，或是只是遭遇惱人的塞車。所有這些事物都會讓我們感到難過或沮喪。在這些時候，冷靜下來並恢復好心情很重要的。以下就是當我感到難過時，改善心情的方法。

　　首先，我告訴自己，無論發生什麼事，都不是世界末日。生命會持續下去，而我最後將會克服困難。然後我會尋找一個解決問題的方式。如果我找到了，我立即採取行動。如果沒有，我會暫時不去想這件事。我已經發現，藉由把我的煩惱和悲傷擱置一旁，我可以有更多精力面對挑戰。因此，我將可以休息一下。我會聽音樂、看電視，或是和朋友聊天。然後，當我心情比較好了，我可以面對我的問題，並解決它們。

　　簡而言之，對我來說，最好激勵我自己的方法，就是暫時不去想我的問題。那樣子，我可以放鬆並有清晰的思慮。然後我就可以找到最好的解決方式。一旦我處理好了問題，我將能夠再次微笑。

*__go through__ 經歷　　fail〔fel〕v. 不及格　　__get caught in__ 遇到
annoying〔ə'nɔɪɪŋ〕adj. 討厭的；煩人的　　__a traffic jam__ 交通阻塞
upset〔ʌp'sɛt〕adj. 不高興的　　__calm down__ 冷靜下來
recover〔rɪ'kʌvɚ〕v. 恢復　　spirits〔'spɪrɪts〕n. pl. 心情；精神
mood〔mud〕n. 心情　　down〔daʊn〕adj. 難過的　　__go on__ 繼續
overcome〔,ovɚ'kʌm〕v. 克服　　eventually〔ɪ'vɛntʃʊəlɪ〕adv. 最後
__take action__ 採取行動　　__right away__ 立刻
__for a while__ 一會兒；一下子　　__put aside__ 撇開不理；不考慮
trouble〔'trʌbl̩〕n. 煩惱　　sorrow〔'saro〕n. 悲傷
energy〔'ɛnɚdʒɪ〕n. 活力　　face〔fes〕v. 面對
challenge〔'tʃælɪndʒ〕n. 挑戰　　therefore〔'ðɛr,for〕adv. 因此
__take a break__ 休息一下　　__in short__ 總之
__cheer__ sb. __up__ 使某人高興起來；激勵某人　　__that way__ 那樣一來
solution〔sə'luʃən〕n. 解決之道　　__deal with__ 應付；處理

92年學測作文範例①

提示：　請以 "Music Is an Important Part of Our Life" 爲題，說明音樂
　　　　（例如古典音樂、流行歌曲、搖滾音樂等）在生活中的重要性，
　　　　並以你或他人的經驗爲例，敘述音樂所帶來的好處。

Music Is an Important Part of Our Life

There is no denying that music plays an important role in everyone's life. It is not only an important art form, but also something that affects our feelings. Attending a concert by professional musicians can help us see and appreciate the beauty of life, while humming a simple tune can help us forget our cares. *In addition*, music always plays a symbolic role at important events such as weddings and graduations. It can put us in the proper mood to enjoy the events.

Music affects my own life in many ways. *First of all*, I play a musical instrument, the piano. I try to spend some time practicing the piano every day. Playing it helps me relax and also gives me a feeling of accomplishment. *Second*, I enjoy listening to music, especially when I feel sad or discouraged. Listening to music can always help me forget my troubles and improve my mood. *Finally*, I like to sing with my friends or family at a KTV. It is a wonderful way to spend free time and it brings us all closer together.

In conclusion, music is important in my life because it relaxes me and makes me happy. *Furthermore*, I believe that music can bring joy to everyone's life. That is why I cannot imagine a world without music.

音樂是我們生命中一個重要的部分

無可否認，音樂在每個人的生命中扮演一個重要的角色。它不只是個藝術形式，也是個會影響我們感受的事物。看一場專業音樂家的音樂會可以幫助我們看到並欣賞生命的美，而哼唱一首簡單的歌曲可以幫助我們忘記擔憂。此外，在重要的活動上，像是婚禮和畢業典禮，音樂總是扮演一個象徵性的角色。它能夠使我們進入一個可以好好享受活動的心情。

音樂影響我生活的許多面向。首先，我彈的樂器是鋼琴。我每天嘗試花一些時間練習鋼琴。彈鋼琴幫助我放鬆，並給我成就感。第二，我喜歡聽音樂，特別是當我難過或沮喪的時候。最後，我喜歡和我的朋友或家人一起在KTV唱歌。這是個度過休閒時光的好方法，而且這讓我們更親近。

總之，音樂在我的生命中很重要，因為它讓我放鬆，使我快樂。此外，我相信音樂可以為每個人的生活帶來愉快。那就是為何我無法想像一個沒有音樂的世界。

---

* ***there's no denying that~*** 不可否認　　form〔fɔrm〕*n.* 型式
affect〔əˈfɛkt〕*v.* 影響　　attend〔əˈtɛnd〕*v.* 參加
concert〔ˈkɑnsɝt〕*n.* 音樂會　　professional〔prəˈfɛʃənl̩〕*adj.* 專業的
appreciate〔əˈpriʃɪˌet〕*v.* 欣賞；了解　　hum〔hʌm〕*v.* 低聲哼唱
tune〔tjun〕*n.* 曲調；旋律　　care〔kɛr〕*n.* 擔憂的事
in addition 此外　　symbolic〔sɪmˈbɑlɪk〕*adj.* 象徵性的
event〔ɪˈvɛnt〕*n.* 重大事件；活動
graduation〔ˌgrædʒuˈeʃən〕*n.* 畢業　　proper〔ˈprɑpɚ〕*adj.* 適當的
mood〔mud〕*n.* 心情　　***musical instrument*** 樂器
accomplishment〔əˈkɑmplɪʃmənt〕*n.* 成就

discouraged〔dɪs'kɝɪdʒd〕*adj.* 沮喪的
improve〔ɪm'pruv〕*v.* 改善；使好轉
furthermore〔'fɝðəˌmor〕*adv.* 此外

troubles〔'trʌblz〕*n. pl.* 煩惱
in conclusion 總之
imagine〔ɪ'mædʒɪn〕*v.* 想像

91年學測作文範例②

提示： 以 "Growing up is a/an _____ experience" 爲題寫一篇英文
作文，描述你成長的經驗是令人興奮的（exciting），令人困惑的
（confusing），快樂的（happy）或是痛苦的（painful）。除了
這些形容詞之外，你也可以用其他的形容詞來描述你成長的經驗。
請務必提出具體的例子以描述你成長的經驗。（注意：如果你用
的形容詞以子音起始，請選擇冠詞 "a"，如 "a confusing
experience"；如果你用的形容詞以母音起始，請選擇冠詞 "an"，
如 "an exciting experience"。

Growing Up Is a Rewarding Experience

There is a great difference between children and adults.
Indeed, all of us will change significantly as we move from
childhood to adulthood. This process is called growing up. It
may be happy at some times and painful at others. It may be
exciting, confusing or frustrating. *Most likely*, it will be all
of these things. *But* for me, the process has been, over all,
rewarding, because as I have matured, I have developed
physically, mentally and emotionally. *Overall*, when I look
back on my childhood and see how much I have advanced, I feel
a great sense of achievement.

Growing up made me more independent and confident. When I was younger, I would not have been capable of, and never would have dared to, take on a lot of responsibility. ***But recently*** I have done just that. Last month, my grandmother fell ill and my mother went back to her hometown to care for her. ***At the time***, my father was overseas on business. I was left in charge of the house and my younger brother and sister. ***At first*** I was afraid I was not up to the challenge. ***But*** I soon found that I could handle the responsibility well. I felt proud of myself. ***Best of all***, my parents said they were proud of me, too. Now they see me as a young adult instead of a child, and that is very rewarding to me.

長大是個有益的經驗

孩童和大人有很大的差異。的確,我們從童年到成人的階段會改變很大。這個過程就稱作成長。這可能有時候是快樂的,而有時候是痛苦的。這可能是令人興奮的、困惑的,或是挫折的。非常有可能的是,這全部都會有。但對我而言,整體來說,這過程是值得的,因爲當我成熟了,我在身體上、心智上,和情感上也成長了。整體來說,當我回頭看我的童年,並看到我有多大的成長,我覺得巨大的成就感。

成長讓我更獨立和有自信。當我比較年輕的時候,我不能夠,也不敢去承擔很多責任。但是最近我才能做到。上個月,我祖母生病了,而我母親回到家鄉去照顧她。在這時候,我父親到海外出差。我留下來看家和照顧的我妹妹和弟弟。一開始我很害怕我無法勝任這樣的挑戰,但我很快發現我可以妥善處理這樣的任務。我感到很自豪,不過最好的是,我父母也說他們爲我感到榮幸。現在他們不再把我看成是孩童，而是個小大人，而那就是我覺得值得的地方。

 * rewarding〔rɪˋwɔrdɪŋ〕*adj.* 有益的；值得的
   significantly〔sɪgˋnɪfəkəntlɪ〕*adv.* 相當大地
   move〔muv〕*v.* 進展；發展　　adulthood〔əˋdʌlt,hud〕*n.* 成年期
   process〔ˋprɑsɛs〕*n.* 過程　　painful〔ˋpenfəl〕*adj.* 痛苦的
   frustrating〔ˋfrʌs,tretɪŋ〕*adj.* 令人沮喪的
   over all 整體而言（= *overall*）
   mature〔məˋtʃur〕*v.* 成熟　　physically〔ˋfɪzɪklɪ〕*adv.* 身體上
   mentally〔ˋmɛntḷɪ〕*adj.* 智力上；心理上
   emotionally〔ɪˋmoʃənḷɪ〕*adv.* 情緒上　　***look back on*** 回顧
   advance〔ədˋvæns〕*v.* 提升；進步
   achievement〔əˋtʃivmənt〕*n.* 成就　　***a sense of achievement*** 成就感
   be capable of 能夠　　***dare to V.*** 敢～　　***take on*** 承擔
   hometown〔ˋhomˋtaun〕*n.* 故鄉　　***care for*** 照顧
   overseas〔ˋovɚˋsiz〕*adv.* 在國外　　***on business*** 因公；出差
   in charge of 負責照料　　***be up to*** 能勝任
   challenge〔ˋtʃælɪndʒ〕*n.* 挑戰　　handle〔ˋhændḷ〕*v.* 處理
   see A ***as*** B 把 A 看作是 B　　***instead of*** 而不是

✎ 91年學測作文範例①

提示：以 "The Most Precious Thing in My Room" 為題寫一篇英文作文，描述你的房間內一件你最珍愛的物品，同時並說明珍愛的理由。（這一件你最珍愛的物品不一定是貴重的，但對你來說卻是最有意義或是最值得紀念的。）

The Most Precious Thing in My Room

　　My room is a special and important place to me. I spend a lot of time there studying, and I also like to relax in my room by listening to music or reading a novel. ***Therefore***, I have taken care to make my room an attractive and comfortable place. I have decorated it with posters of my favorite singers and sports stars. I have also equipped it with a comfortable desk and a good computer on which to do my homework. *However*, the one thing in my room that is most precious to me is a photograph.

This photograph is of my junior high school basketball team. It is precious to me for several reasons. *First*, it reminds me of the good times I had in junior high and the good friendships I had there. I still keep in touch with some of my teammates and we continue to challenge and encourage each other. *Second*, because the photo was taken after our team had won the championship game, it is a symbol of achievement. We were the underdogs that year, and so the photograph reminds me that it is possible to achieve anything with determination and hard work. *Finally*, the photo reminds me that there is more to life than study. Although I have to work hard now, I still make time to relax by playing a game of basketball with good friends.

我房間裡最珍貴的東西

　　我的房間對我來說是個很特別且很重要的地方。我花很多時間在房間裡讀書，而且我也喜歡在房間裡休息，聽音樂或是讀小說。因此，我一直很注意要使我的房間成為一個吸引人又舒服的地方。我用我最喜愛的歌手和運動明星的海報來佈置房間。我的房間也備有舒服的書桌和一台很好的電腦讓我做功課。然而，我房間裡面對我最珍貴的東西是一張相片。

這是我高中籃球隊的照片。這對我很珍貴，有好幾個理由。首先，它讓我想起我高中的美好時光，以及我在籃球隊所擁有的良好友誼。我依然和一些隊友保持聯絡，而且我們持續挑戰和鼓勵彼此。第二，因為這張照片是我們隊贏得冠軍賽的時候照的，它象徵成就。我們那一年並不被看好，所以這張照片提醒了我，有決心和努力就可能完成任何事情。最後，這張照片提醒我，生命不只有讀書。雖然我現在很用功，我依然挪出時間休息，和好朋友打場籃球賽。

* ***take care*** 當心；注意　　decorate〔ˈdɛkəˌret〕*v.* 裝飾；佈置
  poster〔ˈpostɚ〕*n.* 海報　　sports〔spɔrts〕*adj.* 運動的
  equip〔ɪˈkwɪp〕*v.* 裝備；配備 < *with* >
  remind〔rɪˈmaɪnd〕*v.* 使想起 < *of* >
  keep in touch with *sb.* 與某人保持連絡
  teammate〔ˈtimˌmet〕*n.* 隊友　　challenge〔ˈtʃælɪndʒ〕*v.* 向～挑戰
  symbol〔ˈsɪmbḷ〕*n.* 象徵　　achievement〔əˈtʃivmənt〕*n.* 成就
  underdog〔ˈʌndɚˌdɔg〕*n.* 處於劣勢的一方
  determination〔dɪˌtɝməˈneʃən〕*n.* 決心　　***make time*** 騰出時間

✏️ 90年學測作文範例

提示：　請以 "Something Interesting about a Classmate of Mine" 為題，寫出有關你一位同學的一件趣事。這位同學可以是你任何時期的同學，例如中學、小學或幼稚園的同學。

Something Interesting about a Classmate of Mine

Something interesting happened to a classmate of mine, Peter, two years ago. This incident was so funny and interesting that it has left a lasting impression on me. Peter is a normal kid like everyone else, but what had happened to him in class still brings me a good laugh whenever I think about it.

This happened when we were just freshmen. On a sunny afternoon, we were having a lecture on the fine and wonderful history of our great nation. This lesson was important because we needed to know the history of our country, as our teacher said. *However*, he had failed to mention that the lesson would be tediously boring. *Needless to say*, all the students were struggling to stay awake. *Halfway through the class*, Peter let out a shriek which scared all of us into wakefulness. With about fifty pairs of eyes on him, Peter tried to look as normal as he could; *however*, it was very hard to conceal his red face. *It turned out that* Peter had dozed off and had fallen onto his pen which he had held inverted.

I was sure that the teachers appreciated the positive aspect which this incident had brought, because after this embarrassing experience, Peter never fell asleep in class again. *And* I've learned to never hold a pen inverted during a boring class.

我同班同學一件有趣的事

　　兩年前，有件有趣的事發生在我的一個同班同學身上，他叫彼得。這件事是如此好笑又有趣，而在我心中留下揮之不去的印象。彼得是個一般的孩童，跟其他人一樣，但是在上課時候發生在他身上的事情，每當我想起來，依然會大笑一番。

　　這發生在我們還是高一的時候。在一個晴朗的下午，我們正在上一堂課，是關於我們偉大國家的美好歷史。這堂課很重要，因爲我們必須知道我們國家的歷史，我們老師這麼說。不過，他沒有提到這堂課會無聊乏味。不用說，所有的學生都很努力要保持清醒。課上到一半的時候，彼得發出一聲尖叫，嚇得我們全部都醒了過來。有五十雙眼睛看著他，彼得試著盡可能看起來沒有異狀；然而，要掩蓋他紅通通的臉很困難。結果發現，彼得打了瞌睡，並且倒在自己顚倒的筆上。

　　我確定老師們很感激這事件帶來的優點，因爲在這尷尬的經驗後，彼得在課堂上沒有再睡著過。而我學會不在無聊的課堂上握著顚倒的筆。

UNIT 8

* incident〔ˈɪnsədənt〕*n.* 事件　　lasting〔ˈlæstɪŋ〕*adj.* 持久的
impression〔ɪmˈprɛʃən〕*n.* 印象
normal〔ˈnɔrml̩〕*adj.* 普通的；正常的　　lecture〔ˈlɛktʃɚ〕*n.* 講課
tediously〔ˈtidɪəslɪ〕*adv.* 令人乏味地　　***needless to say*** 不用說
struggle〔ˈstrʌgl̩〕*v.* 掙扎；努力　　***stay awake*** 保持清醒
let out 發出　　shriek〔ʃrik〕*n.* 尖叫
wakefulness〔ˈwekfəlnɪs〕*n.* 清醒　　conceal〔kənˈsil〕*v.* 隱藏
doze off 打瞌睡　　invert〔ɪnˈvɝt〕*v.* 顚倒
appreciate〔əˈpriʃɪˌet〕*v.* 感激
aspect〔ˈæspɛkt〕*n.* 方面　　***positive aspect*** 優點

📝89年學測作文範例

提示：　請寫一篇英文作文，主題爲 "Weight Loss"：以你個人或你熟悉
　　　　的人（朋友、親戚）爲例，說明造成這個人體重過重的原因，並
　　　　提出你認爲理想的解決之道。

Weight Loss

Obesity is a common problem for people of all ages
and walks of life. *Take* my obese friend Laura *for example*,

she eats fast food virtually every day and never fails to include sweets for desserts. Once she gets home, she turns into a couch potato. You can hardly get her to move once she sits on her favorite chair and starts devouring a bag of potato chips. *Moreover*, she is too lazy to walk, not to mention taking the stairs.

Obesity is not a problem that can be solved overnight. You cannot simply turn yourself into the likes of Arnold Schwarzenegger or Catherine Zeta Jones the moment you decide you want an improved figure. *In other words*, you have to work hard for it. Although there are now drugs and clinical methods that claim to help solve the problem of obesity, they are not wonder drugs that promise guaranteed and lasting results. *Instead*, you must have patience, self-discipline and determination if you want to trim down the excess weight. *In closing*, professionals in this field continue to say that regular exercise, a well-balanced diet, keeping regular hours and avoiding junk food and sweets remain the best way.

減　重

　　肥胖對所有年齡和行業的人來說，是個常見的問題。拿我肥胖的朋友蘿拉作例子，她幾乎每天都吃速食，而且一定會吃甜食作甜點。一回到家，她就躺在沙發上看電視。一旦她坐在她最喜歡的椅子上，並開始狼吞虎嚥地吃整袋的馬鈴薯片，你就很難讓她動起來。此外，她很懶惰，不願意走路，更不用說爬樓梯了。

　　肥胖不是短時間可以解決的問題。你無法在你決定要改善你身材那一刻，就輕易地把你自己變成像是阿諾・史瓦辛格，或凱薩琳・麗塔瓊絲之類的人。換言之，你必須努力才能達成。雖然有很多藥物和臨床的方法，宣稱能幫助解決體重過重的問題，它們不是萬靈丹，可以保證持久的效果。反而，如果你要消除過多的體重，你必須要有耐心、自律，和決心。總之，這領域的專家一直說，規律的運動、均衡的飲食、早睡早起，並避免垃圾食物和甜食，依然是最好的方法。

---

* obesity〔o'bisətɪ〕 *n.* 肥胖　　　***walk of life*** 職業

obese〔o'bis〕 *adj.* 極肥胖的　　　virtually〔'vɜtʃʊəlɪ〕 *adv.* 實際上

fail〔fel〕 *v.* 沒有　　　sweets〔swits〕 *n. pl.* 甜食

dessert〔dɪ'zɜt〕 *n.* 甜點　　***turn into*** 變成

couch potato 躺在沙發上看電視的懶人

devour〔dɪ'vaʊr〕 *v.* 吞食；狼吞虎嚥地吃

potato chips （油炸的）馬鈴薯片　　***not to mention*** 更不用說

take the stairs 爬樓梯　　overnight〔'ovə'naɪt〕 *adj.* 短時間的

the likes of ~ 類似~之人或物　　figure〔'fɪgə〕 *n.* 身材

clinical〔'klɪnɪkḷ〕 *adj.* 臨床的　　claim〔klem〕 *v.* 聲稱

wonder drug 仙丹；萬靈藥　　guaranteed〔ˌgærən'tid〕 *adj.* 保證的

lasting〔'læstɪŋ〕 *adj.* 持久的　　self-discipline〔'sɛlf'dɪsəplɪn〕 *n.* 自制

determination〔dɪˌtɜmə'neʃən〕 *n.* 決心　　trim〔trɪm〕 *v.* 削減

excess〔ɪk'sɛs〕 *adj.* 多餘的　　field〔fild〕 *n.* 領域

well-balanced〔'wɛl'bælənst〕 *adj.* 均衡的　　diet〔'daɪət〕 *n.* 飲食

keep regular hours 生活有規律　　***junk food*** 垃圾食物

📝88年學測作文範例

提示：　根據以上四則求職廣告，寫一篇英文作文。文分兩段：第一段寫出你認為這四種工作中那一種對你而言是最好的工作，並說明理由；第二段則寫出四種工作中你最不可能選擇的工作，也說明理由。假如這四種工作你都不喜歡，則在第一段說明都不喜歡的理由，在第二段寫你喜歡什麼工作，並說明理由。

A

MARKETING PROFESSIONALS

A major US corporation in the health and nutritional industry has announced the opening of its direct sales division in Taiwan.

The company offers the most lucrative compensation plan in the industry and has paid over $*3.5 billion NTD in commissions* in just 6 years in the US. We are a group of top earners.

Applicants should meet these requirements:
(1) Taiwan citizen
(2) Have interest or experience in marketing
(3) Aggressive, energetic, and willing to learn

If you believe you have what it takes to develop this business, please call 2742-6996

B

An international company requires a

Service Technician

to service and maintain electronic medical equipment.
Applicants should possess a degree in electronics.
The selected candidate will undergo a training program to be conducted by our manufacturer's trained technical personnel.

Interested candidates please apply immediately by mail with resume to P.O. box 594. Or telephone Ms. Chang at 2945-0027 for an immediate interview.

C

Wanted: Reporters & Editors

Qualifications:
※ Strong command of English
※ Chinese speaking and reading ability a must
※ a university degree
※ Journalism education and/or experience a plus

Flexible working hours (30 hours per week)
Good work environment and great co-workers
Medical insurance, etc.

Fax resume and work samples, if any, to The China Post at (03) 2595-7962.

D

Southeastern Travel Services

OPENINGS ************************
TOUR GUIDES

Duties: To conduct escorted tours for foreign visitors; to assist with travel and transportation arrangements.

Qualifications: Good appearance. High school diploma. Good knowledge of English. Outgoing personality.

Call 2703-2172 after 3:00 PM. Ask for Gary.

A

MARKETING PROFESSIONALS

A major US corporation in the health and nutritional industry has announced the opening of its direct sales division in Taiwan.

The company offers the most lucrative compensation plan in the industry and has paid over $3.5 billion NTD in commissions in just 6 years in the US. We are a group of top earners.

Applicants should meet these requirements:
(1) Taiwan citizen
(2) Have interest or experience in marketing
(3) Aggressive, energetic, and willing to learn

If you believe you have what it takes to develop
this business, please call 2742-6996

A.

行銷專員

美國一家健康營養業的大公司，已宣布在台灣的直銷部門開張。

公司提供同業中利潤最豐厚的薪資計劃，在美國僅僅六年，就已付出新台幣三十五億以上的佣金。我們是一群高薪者。

申請人應要符合以下資格：

(1) 台灣公民
(2) 對行銷有興趣或經驗
(3) 積極、有活力，願意學習

如果你相信你具有發展本行的條件，請電 2742-6996。

* marketing ('markɪtɪŋ) *n.* 行銷　　corporation (,kɔrpə'reʃən) *n.* 公司
nutritional (nju'trɪʃənḷ) *adj.* 營養的　　announce (ə'naʊns) *v.* 宣布
division (də'vɪʒən) *n.* 部門　　lucrative ('lukrətɪv) *adj.* 有利潤的
compensation (,kampən'seʃən) *n.* 薪水；津貼

commission〔kəˋmɪʃən〕*n.* 佣金　　applicant〔ˋæpləkənt〕*n.* 申請人
requirement〔rɪˋkwaɪrmənt〕*n.* 資格；條件
aggressive〔əˋgrɛsɪv〕*adj.* 積極進取的

B

An international company requires a

Service Technician

to service and maintain electronic medical equipment.

Applicants should possess a degree in electronics. The
selected candidate will undergo a training program to be
conducted by our manufacturer's trained technical
personnel.

Interested candidates please apply immediately by mail
with resume to P.O. box 594. Or telephone Ms. Chang at
2945-0027 for an immediate interview.

B.

跨國企業需要一名

維修技師

來維修、保養電子醫療器材。

申請人應具有電子學的學位。入選者將接受由我們製造商受過訓
練的技術人員所指導的訓練課程。

有興趣者請立刻備履歷應徵，郵寄至郵政信箱 594 號。或請電
2945-0027，找張小姐，安排立即面試。

＊service〔ˋsɝvɪs〕*n., v.* 服務；維修
technician〔tɛkˋnɪʃən〕*n.* 技師；技術人員
maintain〔menˋten〕*v.* 維修；保養　　possess〔pəˋzɛs〕*v.* 擁有
electronics〔͵ɪlɛkˋtrɑnɪks〕*n.* 電子學

candidate〔'kændə,det,'kændədɪt〕*n.* 候選人
undergo〔,ʌndə'go〕*v.* 經歷　　conduct〔kən'dʌkt〕*v.* 指導；領導
technical〔'tɛknɪkl̩〕*adj.* 技術的　　personnel〔,pɜsn̩'ɛl〕*n.* 人員
resume〔,rɛzu'me,,rɛzju'me〕*n.* 履歷　　***P.O. box*** 郵政信箱

C

Wanted: Reporters & Editors

Qualifications:

※ Strong command of English

※ Chinese speaking and reading ability a must

※ a university degree

※ Journalism education and/or experience a plus

Flexible working hours (30 hours per week)
Good work environment and great co-workers
Medical insurance, etc.

Fax resume and work samples, if any, to
The China Post at (03) 2595-7962.

C.

誠徵：記者&編輯

資格：

% 精通英文

% 中文說與讀的能力必備條件

% 大學學歷

% 新聞學教育以及／或經驗附加優點

彈性工時（每週三十小時）
良好的工作環境，優秀的工作同仁
享醫療保險等。

請傳眞履歷及作品範例，如果有的話，

至中國英文郵報 (03) 2595-7962。

* qualification〔ˌkwɑləfəˈkeʃən〕*n.* 資格
command〔kəˈmænd〕*n.* 精通　　must〔mʌst〕*n.* 必要的事
journalism〔ˈdʒɜnəlˌɪzəm〕*n.* 新聞學　　plus〔plʌs〕*n.* 附加的優點
flexible〔ˈflɛksəbḷ〕*adj.* 彈性的　　insurance〔ɪnˈʃurəns〕*n.* 保險
sample〔ˈsæmpḷ〕*n.* 範例；樣品

D

Southeastern Travel Services

OPENINGS ***************************

TOUR GUIDES

Duties: To conduct escorted tours for foreign visitors; to assist with travel and transportation arrangements.

Qualifications: Good appearance.　High school diploma. Good knowledge of English.　Outgoing personality.

Call 2703-2172 after 3:00 PM.　Ask for Gary.

D.

東南旅行社

空缺 **************************

導遊

職務：帶領有接送的外國旅行團；協助安排旅遊及交通事宜。

資格：長相清秀。高中文憑。擅長英文。個性外向。

電 2703-2172，下午三點後，找 Gary。

* escort〔ɪˈskɔrt〕*v.* 護送　　assist〔əˈsɪst〕*v.* 協助

transportation〔͵trænspə'teʃən〕*n.* 交通（工具）
arrangement〔ə'rendʒmənt〕*n.* 安排　　diploma〔dɪ'plomə〕*n.* 文憑
outgoing〔aʊt'goɪŋ〕*adj.* 外向的

　　With my personal qualities and travel experience, I
believe I am well-qualified for the position of tour guide.
Being young, bright and energetic, I don't like to work in a
cubicle with a fixed schedule.　Having the ability to get along
with people with different interests and backgrounds, I get
used to a new environment quickly.　*Furthermore*, I have
traveled throughout Europe and America on my own.　A
variety of emergencies and problems I've encountered and
overcome have taught me how to deal with sickness, criminal
incidents, and culture shock.　*Therefore*, I'm sure that my
personal background and multi-lingual ability, which includes
English, Spanish and Chinese, will help me handle any
hazard which my tour group might face.

　　A service technician is the last job that I wish to apply
for.　*Besides* lacking the relevant academic background, I care
nothing about electronics.　*Moreover*, this kind of job cannot
provide challenge and freedom where I can use my initiative
and creativity.　*To sum up*, in choosing an
occupation, one has to consider his/her aptitude above all, or
working is a burden, instead of fun.

　　以我個人特質和旅行經驗，我相信我非常適合導遊這個職位。年輕、開朗、有活力，我不喜歡在小房間做規律的工作。我有能力和不同興趣及背景的人相處，並且很快能習慣新的環境。此外，我獨自旅行過歐洲和美國。我遭遇過各種緊急狀況和問題，這些教導我如何處理疾病、犯罪事件，以及文化衝擊。因此，我確定我個人的背景和多語言的能力，包含英文、西班牙文，和中文，將能幫助我處理任何我的旅行團可能會面臨的危險。

　　維修技師是我最不希望應徵的工作。除了缺少相關的學術背景，我完全不想理會電子學。另外，這種工作無法給我挑戰和自由，讓我發揮我的進取心和創意。總而言之，在選擇工作時，最重要的是，一個人必須考慮他或她的性向，否則工作是負擔，不是樂趣。

UNIT 8

*quality〔ˋkwɑlətɪ〕n. 特質　　position〔pəˋzɪʃən〕n. 職位
bright〔braɪt〕adj. 開朗的；聰明的
cubicle〔ˋkjubɪkḷ〕n. 小房間
get along with～　與～相處　　**a variety of** 各種
emergency〔ɪˋmɝdʒənsɪ〕n. 緊急情況
encounter〔ɪnˋkaʊntə〕v. 遭遇　　overcome〔͵ovəˋkʌm〕v. 克服
deal with 處理（= handle）　　criminal〔ˋkrɪmənḷ〕adj. 犯罪的
incident〔ˋɪnsədnt〕n. 事件　　**culture shock** 文化衝擊
multi-lingual〔͵mʌltəˋlɪŋgwəl〕adj. 多語的；會說多種語言的
hazard〔ˋhæzəd〕n. 危險（= danger）
relevant〔ˋrɛləvənt〕adj. 相關的
academic〔͵ækəˋdɛmɪk〕adj. 學術的
care nothing about 不關心；不在乎
challenge〔ˋtʃælɪndʒ〕n. 挑戰
initiative〔ɪˋnɪʃɪ͵etɪv〕n. 主動；進取
creativity〔͵krieˋtɪvətɪ〕n. 創意；創造力
to sum up 總之　　occupation〔͵ɑkjəˋpeʃən〕n. 職業
aptitude〔ˋæptə͵tjud〕n. 性向　　burden〔ˋbɝdn̩〕n. 負擔

📝87年學測作文範例

提示：每個人在不同的情況下對雨可能有不同的感受。請寫一篇短文，敘述你在某一個下雨天的實際經歷或看到的景象，並據此描述你對雨的感覺。

I have had many rainy day experiences. Just recently, one such experience happened. It was a sunny day, and I was on my way to my friend's birthday party. Because of the sun, I didn't think an umbrella was necessary. *Unfortunately*, I found out that I had made a big mistake. Dressed in my best clothes, I got caught in a sudden downpour. It was so heavy, and came so fast, that there was no way for me to escape it. *Moreover*, I had no time to go back and change, so I continued on. *Consequently*, I arrived soaking wet, and had to stand in a puddle throughout the party.

Despite the inconveniences brought about by rain, it can bring me great joy and happiness. I love flowers very much, and without rain, they wouldn't be possible. *What's better*, the rain also cleans the air and brings coolness on hot summer days, which helps to make life in Taiwan a little more bearable. Like everything, rain has a good side and a bad side. I've learned to live with the bad side, and quite enjoy the good side. *Therefore*, let it rain.

　　我曾經經歷過許多雨天。這樣的經驗發生在最近。那天是晴天，而我正在前往朋友生日派對的路上。因為有陽光，我不覺得有必要帶雨傘。很不幸的，我發現我犯了大錯。穿著我最好的衣服，我被突如其來的傾盆大雨淋濕。雨下得又大又急，以致於我沒有辦法能躲雨。此外，我沒有時間回去換衣服，所以我繼續前往。因此，我到的時候全身濕透，且整場派對中得站在積水處。

　　儘管雨帶來不便，它也帶來了極大的快樂和幸福。我非常喜歡花，而沒有雨，就不可能有花。更好的是，雨也淨化了空氣，並給炎熱的夏日帶來涼爽，這也幫助了讓台灣的生活稍微可以忍受。跟所有事物一樣，雨有好處也有壞的一面。我已經學到了和不好的一面共處，並好好地享受優點。所以，讓雨落下吧。

* downpour〔ˈdaʊnˌpor〕n. 傾盆大雨　　　soak〔sok〕v. 濕透
　 puddle〔ˈpʌdḷ〕n.（雨後）積水處
　 bearable〔ˈbɛrəbḷ〕adj. 可忍受的

📝 86年學測作文範例

提示：

　　你同意 "Laughter is better than medicine" 這種說法嗎？<u>以你自己或親朋好友的經驗或你所知道的故事為例</u>，加以說明。你的論點無論是正面或是反面都不會影響你的得分。

Laughter Is Better than Medicine

　　A friend of mine, Julia, was once hospitalized. *At first* she stayed in a room all by herself. She felt so depressed and had no appetite at all. She looked worse than before, even though she was taking medicine regularly. *Then* her mother moved her to another room which she shared with other patients. One of them always told jokes and made them all laugh. In two days, Julia changed completely. Not only did she look happy, but her health also improved. *Thus*, she checked out of the hospital earlier than the doctor expected.

Medicine is used to cure all kinds of illnesses; *however*, there are some situations where medicine just can't help. When we are nervous, or in low spirits, a good laugh can relieve our tension and put us in a better mood. Laughter sometimes works like a miracle, doing wonders for both physical and mental health. *Therefore*, I truly believe that laughter is really better than any other medicine.

UNIT 8

笑 比 藥 有 效

我有一個朋友叫朱莉亞,曾經住院。一開始她自己待在一個房間。她覺得很難過,而且完全沒有食慾。她看起來比之前還糟糕,即使她規律吃藥。然後她母親把她移到另一個房間,和其他病人一起住。其中一個病人總是說說笑話,使他們所有人大笑。兩天後,朱莉亞完全改變了。她不只看起來很快樂,她的健康也改善了。因此,她比醫生預期的早出院。

藥物是用來治療各種疾病,然而,有些情況是藥物無法幫得上忙。當我們緊張的時候,或是心情低落時,大笑一番可以減輕壓力,讓我們心情變好。笑有時候有奇蹟的功效,對身體和心靈的健康有驚人的效果。因此,我深信笑真的筆任何其他藥物有效。

* hospitalize (ˈhɑspɪtḷˌaɪz) v. 使住院　　appetite (ˈæpəˌtaɪt) n. 食慾
regularly (ˈrɛgjələlɪ) adv. 定期地　　move (muv) v. 遷移
share with~ 與~共用　　　**check out** 付帳離開
be in low spirits 心情不好　　**relieve one's tension** 消除緊張
mood (mud) n. 心情　　miracle (ˈmɪrəkḷ) n. 奇蹟
do wonders 產生驚人的效果；（藥）有奇效

✍️ 85年學測作文範例

背景提示：

　　西元 1939 年紐約世界博覽會前夕，主辦單位在會址的地底下埋了一個時間膠囊（ time capsule ），裡面放了許多最能代表當時生活方式的物品，如電話機、開罐器、手錶、香煙、以及一塊煤炭等。這個密封的盒要等到西元 6939 年才打開，以便讓五千年後的人知道 1930 年代的生活型態。

　　現在有一個國際性基金會也預備舉辦類似的活動，要將一個真空密閉的時間膠囊埋在地底，膠囊中的東西都不會腐壞，好讓一千年以後的人知道 1996 年世界各地區的生活方式。該基金會公開向各國人士徵求建議。

提示：

　　請你寫一篇英文短文前往應徵，提出最能代表我國人民生活現狀的物品兩件（體積不限），說明你選擇這兩件物品的理由，並以 "The two things I would like to put in the time capsule are..." 作為短文的開頭。

　　The two things I would like to put in the time capsule are a personal computer and an abacus, to indicate where we are going as well as where we have been. Here in the Far East things are changing at an accelerated pace. Nothing symbolizes this better than the computer, which has possibly even encroached upon our lives. ***On the other hand***, the abacus reminds us of quieter times in stark contrast with present-day traffic jams accompanied by the incessant blaring of horns.

I want my time capsule to help future generations understand the contradictions so prevalent in modern Chinese society. *For one thing*, it will give them a better perspective than the ubiquitous "scorecards" brandished by activists and sensationalist reporters. *For another*, we must not look at only one aspect of Chinese culture, like a racehorse with blinkers put on it. If this can help future historians clarify misunderstanding, it will be worth the effort.

UNIT 8

　　我想要放進時空膠囊的兩項物品是個人電腦和算盤，爲了要表示我們進展到哪裡，以及我們經歷過的階段。在遠東這地方，事物加速在改變中，而且沒有事物可以比電腦更佳象徵這樣的情況，因爲根據某些人的看法，電腦甚至侵佔了我們的生活。另一方面來說，算盤讓我們想起更寧靜的時光，對比現今的塞車和不斷發出鳴響的喇叭。

　　我希望我的時空膠囊可以幫助未來的世代了解當代中國社會普遍的矛盾。其一，比起激進主義者和譁眾取寵的記者，他們所到處揮舞的「計分卡」，這將讓他們有更整體的了解。其二，我們不該選擇只看現在中國文化的一個部分，這樣就像是戴著眼罩的賽馬。如果這可以幫助未來的歷史學家澄清誤會，這努力就值得了。

UNIT 8

* abacus〔ˈæbəkəs〕*n.* 算盤　　***Far East*** 遠東

accelerate〔ækˈsɛləˌret〕*v.* 加速　　pace〔pes〕*n.* 速度；步調

symbolize〔ˈsɪmbḷˌaɪz〕*v.* 象徵　　encroach〔ɪnˈkrotʃ〕*v.* 侵佔

remind *sb.* ***of*** *sth.* 提醒某人某事；使某人想起某事

stark〔stɑrk〕*adj.* 完全的

contrast〔ˈkɑntræst〕*n.* 對比；反襯

accompany〔əˈkʌmpənɪ〕*v.* 伴隨

incessant〔ɪnˈsɛsṇt〕*adj.* 不停的　　blaring〔ˈblɛrɪŋ〕*n.* 發出聲音

horn〔hɔrn〕*n.*（汽車的）喇叭

future〔ˈfjutʃɚ〕*adj.* 未來的　　generation〔ˌdʒɛnəˈreʃən〕*n.* 世代

contradiction〔ˌkɑntrəˈdɪkʃən〕*n.* 矛盾

prevalent〔ˈprɛvələnt〕*adj.* 普遍的

perspective〔pɚˈspɛktɪv〕*n.* 對事物整體的看法

ubiquitous〔juˈbɪkwətəs〕*adj.* 遍布的

scorecard〔ˈskorˌkɑrd〕*n.* 記分卡（比喻為示威者的旗幟、標語）

brandish〔ˈbrændɪʃ〕*v.* 揮動

activist〔ˈæktɪvɪst〕*n.* 活躍分子；實踐主義者

sensationalist〔sɛnˈseʃənḷɪst〕*adj.* 煽情主義的；譁眾取寵的

aspect〔ˈæspɛkt〕*n.* 方面　　racehorse〔ˈresˌhɔrs〕*n.* 賽馬

blinker〔ˈblɪŋkɚ〕*n.* 馬眼罩　　clarify〔ˈklærəˌfaɪ〕*v.* 澄清

📝 84年學測作文範例

提示：

1. 高中生王治平收到美國筆友 George 的來信，告訴治平他要隨父母到
   台灣來住兩年左右，並問治平：“Can you give me some advice and
   suggestions so that I know what I should do and what I should not
   do when I am in Taiwan?” 現在請你以治平的身份，擬一封適當的回
   信給 George，歡迎他來台灣，並且針對他的問題，提出一些具體的
   建議。

2. 回信的上下款應依下列方式寫出。

February 20, 1995

Dear George:

```
------------------------------------------
------------------------------------------
------------------------------------------
------------------------------------------
------------------------------------------
                    .
                    .
                    .
        ----------------------------------
        ----------------------------------
        ----------------------------------
        ----------------------------------
        ----------------------------------
```

Your friend,
Chih-ping

February 20, 1995

Dear George,

I'm really glad to hear that you're coming to Taiwan. During your stay here, you must make good use of the two years to see Taiwan for yourself. Taiwan, *as you already know*, is a mountainous island. *Therefore, the first thing* you should do is pay a visit to our scenic mountains, such as Mt. Ali and Mt. Jade. You will be deeply impressed with the grandeur and magnificence of the mountains. After having enough of the gorgeous scenes, try the food at the local night market. The tasty snacks will make you want one more bite.

But beware of the traffic in big cities. You should avoid the rush hours lest you get stuck in the heavy traffic. When you go out to downtown, take the bus if possible. If you drive, you may find it hard to park. *On the other hand*, when you stroll along the sidewalk, watch out for the blocking motorcycles parked on it. You may bump into one if you are not careful. The traffic in Taiwan is quite different from that in the States. *Finally*, I'm going to say "Welcome to Taiwan." I'm sure you'll find it interesting to live in Taiwan.

Your friend,

Chih-ping

親愛的喬治：

　　我真的很高興聽到你要來台灣了。在你待在這裡的這段期間，你一定要善用這兩年親自看看台灣。就如你所知，台灣是個多山的島。因此，你第一件應該做的就是去參觀風景優美的山，像是阿里山和玉山。你會深受這些山的壯觀和偉大所感動。在看完美麗的景色後，嘗試看看當地的夜市。美味的小吃會讓你一口接一口的吃。

　　不過，要小心大都市的交通。你應該要避免尖峰時刻，以免你困在交通阻塞中。當你到市區時，可能的話，搭公車。如果你開車，你可能會發現很難停車。另一方面，當你在人行道散步時，小心停在人行道擋路的摩托車。如果你不小心的話，你可能會撞倒。台灣的交通和美國非常不同。最後，我要說：「歡迎來到台灣。」我確定你會覺得住在台灣很有趣。

你的朋友，
志平
1995年2月20日

* **make (good) use of** （好好）利用
mountainous〔'maʊntṇəs〕 *adj.* 多山的
scenic〔'sinɪk,'sɛn-〕 *adj.* 風景優美的　　grandeur〔'grændʒɚ〕 *n.* 壯觀
magnificence〔mæg'nɪfəsṇs〕 *n.* 壯麗
gorgeous〔'gɔrdʒəs〕 *adj.* 極好的　　snack〔snæk〕 *n.* 小吃
beware of 小心～　　**rush hour** 尖峰時間
lest〔lɛst〕 *conj.* 以免　　park *v.* 停車
stroll〔strol〕 *v.* 漫步　　blocking〔'blɑkɪŋ〕 *adj.* 阻擋的

UNIT 8

📝 83年學測作文範例

題目：Things Are Not As Difficult As They Appear

在成長過程中，有些事情在開始的時候你可能覺得很難，但經過一番努力後就不再認為困難了，請寫一篇至少一百二十個單字的英文作文，描述一個親身的經驗。文章的頭兩句必須是：Things are not as difficult as they appear. I have a personal experience to prove this.

Things Are Not As Difficult As They Appear

Things are not as difficult as they appear. *For example*, I have a personal experience to prove this. One day I went hiking in the mountains. Not accustomed to the cold weather and the long trudge, I found it a cruel torment. *Thus*, disheartened and exhausted, I felt I would never reach the top and I could not keep it up for another minute. *However*, having no chance to return, I climbed up step by step and finally reached the top.

When I went downhill, *strangely enough*, I found the path short, even though it was still the same path as before. *However*, this time I had in mind that the destination was approaching. Life is like a long path with adversity. We should not be discouraged by tough appearances from trying many things. Once we have experienced them, we will realize things are never as difficult as they appear. *Therefore*, we can reach our goals if we keep going with perseverance.

UNIT 8

事情不如它們看起來得難

　　事情並不如它們看起來得難。我有一個個人的經驗來證明。有一天我去山區健行。因為不習慣冷的天氣和長途跋涉，我覺得這非常痛苦。因此，既氣餒又疲憊，我覺得我不可能爬到山頂，而且我也無法再堅持一分鐘。然而，沒有機會回頭，我一步一步的爬，而最後到了山頂。

　　當我走下坡的時候，很奇怪的是，我覺得路途很短，即使是走和之前同樣的道路。不過，這一次我牢記在心，目的地就不遠了。生命就像是一條面對逆境的路途。我們不應該因艱困的外觀而感到氣餒，而不去嘗試很多事物。一旦我們經歷過了它們，我們將會了解當事情不如它們看起來得難。因此，如果我們保持毅力，我們就可以達到目標。

---

*trudge〔trʌdʒ〕*n.* 跋涉　　torment〔'tɔrmɛnt〕*n.* 痛苦
dishearten〔dɪs'hɑrtn̩〕*v.* 使氣餒　　***keep it up*** 照目前情形繼續下去
destination〔ˌdɛstə'neʃən〕*n.* 目的地　　approach〔ə'protʃ〕*v.* 接近
adversity〔əd'vɝsətɪ〕*n.* 逆境；惡運
perseverance〔ˌpɝsə'vɪrəns〕*n.* 堅忍；毅力

9 歷屆指考作文範例 ✎

✒ 105年指考作文範例

提示： 最近有一則新聞報導，標題為「碩士清潔隊員（waste collectors with a master's degree）滿街跑」，提及某縣市招考清潔隊員，出現 50 位碩士畢業生報考，引起各界關注。請就這個主題，寫一篇英文作文，文長至少 120 個單詞。文分兩段，第一段依據你的觀察說明這個現象的成因，第二段則就你如何因應上述現象，具體（舉例）說明你對大學生涯的學習規劃。

A Master's Degree in Waste Collection

The main reason why these highly-educated people are willing to be waste collectors is that the job market for highly-educated employees is over-crowded, extremely competitive, and shrinking on a daily basis. *Additionally*, the globalization of the world's economy means that companies have access to equally qualified employees who are willing to work for less money. *For instance*, Disney recently made the news for replacing American workers with foreign nationals who were willing to accept half the compensation of their American counterparts. Corporations answer only to their shareholders, and their primary objective is profit. *Thus*, they don't care who does the job; only that it gets done.

UNIT 9

In my opinion, society in general puts a lot of pressure on people to live up to certain expectations that in reality are unreasonable. *That is to say*, a master's in business administration doesn't guarantee you a job in finance, nor does it automatically make you a good businessperson. My learning plan in college will involve a great deal of flexibility and my studies will include a wide range of subjects. *At the same time*, I have reasonable expectations about my future in the job market. *To be honest*, it sounds like the waste collection industry is booming, and I'm already enrolled in a waste management course. *Besides*, I hear the waste collector job pays pretty well and comes with a number of benefits like health insurance and paid vacation. With a good plan, I am confident that I can secure the right job for me.

UNIT 9

碩士清潔隊員

為何這些高學歷的人願意當清潔隊員,這是因為高學歷員工的就業市場供不應求、非常競爭,而且天天都在萎縮。此外,世界經濟全球化代表著,公司可以接觸到願意接受比較低的工資,卻一樣有能力的員工。例如,迪士尼公司最近發佈新聞,用外國國民取代美國員工,他們願意接受美國員工一半的工資。公司只對股東負責,而他們主要的目標是利潤。因此,他們不在乎誰做工作;只要有人做。

依我之見,社會普遍施加很多壓力在人們身上,要他們達到某些實際上不合理的期待。也就是說,商學管理的碩士學位不能保證你找到金融業的工作,也無法自動讓你能夠成為一位好的商人。我的大學學習計畫將會有很大的彈性，而且我的學業將會包含廣泛的科目。同時，我對我未來在就業市場上有合理的期待。坦白說，現在聽起來垃圾回收產業正在蓬勃發展，而我已經登記了垃圾管理的課程。此外，我聽說清潔隊員的薪水很好，而且附帶有很多福利，像是健康保險和帶薪假。有這樣良好計畫，我有信心我可以爲我自己找到正確的工作。

---

* master ('mæstɚ) n. 碩士　degree (dɪ'gri) n. 學位
waste (west) n. 廢物；垃圾
highly-educated adj. 教育程度高的；高學歷的
willing ('wɪlɪŋ) adj. 有意願的　***job market*** 就業市場；職場
employee (,ɛmplɔɪ'i) n. 受雇者；員工
over-crowded (,ovɚ'kraʊdɪd) adj. 過度擁擠的
extremely (ɪk'strimlɪ) adv. 極度地；非常
competitive (kəm'pɛtətɪv) adj. 競爭激烈的
shrink (ʃrɪŋk) v. 縮小；變小
on a daily basis 每天 (= *every day*)

*　　　　*　　　　*

additionally (ə'dɪʃənḷɪ) adv. 此外 (= *besides*)
globalization (,globəlaɪ'zeʃən) n. 全球化
economy (ɪ'kɑnəmɪ) n. 經濟
access ('æksɛs) n. 接觸；取得；利用
have access to 能取得；能利用　equally ('ikwəlɪ) adv. 同樣地
qualified ('kwɑlə,faɪd) adj. 有資格的
for instance 例如 (= *for example*)
Disney ('dɪznɪ) n. 迪士尼 (公司)
make the news 上新聞　replace (rɪ'ples) v. 取代；替換

*　　　　*　　　　*

foreign ('fɔrɪn) adj. 外國的　national ('næʃənḷ) n. 國民
compensation (,kɑmpən'seʃən) n. 補償；薪水 (= *pay*)
counterpart ('kaʊntɚ,part) n. 相對應的人或物
corporation (,kɔrpə'reʃən) n. 公司
answer ('ænsɚ) v. 回答；負責 < *to* >

shareholder〔'ʃɛr,holdə〕*n.* 股東　　primary〔'praɪ,mɛrɪ〕*adj.* 主要的
objective〔əb'dʒɛktɪv〕*n.* 目標（*= goal*）
profit〔'prɑfɪt〕*n.* 利益；利潤　　thus〔ðʌs〕*adv.* 因此（*= therefore*）
in one's opinion 依某人之見
in general 一般說來；大體而言（*= generally*）
pressure〔'prɛʃə〕*n.* 壓力
live up to 達到；符合（*= meet = fulfill*）　　certain〔'sɜtn̩〕*adj.* 某些
expectation〔,ɛkspɛk'teʃən〕*n.* 期待；期望
in reality 事實上　　unreasonable〔ʌn'riznəbl̩〕*adj.* 不合理的
that is to say 也就是說；換句話說（*= in other words = that is*
　= namely）
business〔'bɪznɪs〕*n.* 商業

＊　　　　　　＊　　　　　　＊

administration〔əd,mɪnə'streʃən〕*n.* 管理
guarantee〔,gærən'ti〕*v.* 保證　　finance〔'faɪnæns〕*n.* 財務
automatically〔,ɔtə'mætɪkl̩ɪ〕*adv.* 自動地；必然
businessperson〔'bɪznɪs,pɜsn̩〕*n.* 商人（*= businessman*）
involve〔ɪn'vɑlv〕*v.* 牽涉；包含　　*a great deal of* 很多；大量的
flexibility〔,flɛksə'bɪlətɪ〕*n.* 彈性　　studies〔'stʌdɪz〕*n. pl.* 課業
range〔redʒ〕*n.* 範圍　　*a wide range of* 廣泛的；各種的
at the same time 同時（*= meanwhile*）
reasonable〔'riznəbl̩〕*adj.* 合理的

＊　　　　　　＊　　　　　　＊

to be honest 老實說（*= honestly speaking*）
industry〔'ɪndəstrɪ〕*n.* 產業　　boom〔bum〕*v.* 繁榮；蓬勃發展
enroll〔ɪn'rol〕*v.* 註冊；參加　　*be enrolled in* 參加；登記
management〔'mænɪdʒmənt〕*n.* 管理
besides〔bɪ'saɪdz〕*adv.* 此外　　*come with* 附帶有
a number of 一些　　benefit〔'bɛnəfɪt〕*n.* 好處；福利
insurance〔ɪn'ʃurəns〕*n.* 保險
health insurance 健康保險　　*paid vacation* 帶薪假
confident〔'kɑnfədənt〕*adj.* 確信的　　secure〔sɪ'kjur〕*v.* 獲得

📝 104年指考作文範例

提示：　指導別人學習讓他學會一件事物，或是得到別人的指導而自己學
　　　　會一件事物，都是很好的經驗。請根據你過去幫助別人學習，或
　　　　得到別人的指導而學會某件事的經驗，寫一篇至少 120 個單詞的
　　　　英文作文。文分兩段，第一段說明該次經驗的緣由、內容和過程，
　　　　第二段說明你對該次經驗的感想。

Helping Others Learn

Just recently, my grandmother decided to buy a computer
so she could get acquainted with the Internet. She's not very
familiar with modern technology, so she asked me to help her
set up the system and get started surfing the web. *First*, I
showed her how to open and use programs on the desktop.
Then I helped her set up an email account. *Finally*, we
downloaded a video conferencing program so she could call
other family members who live in different parts of the world.
All in all, I spent the better part of an afternoon helping
Grandma get acquainted with the Internet.

The experience was very rewarding for a couple of
reasons. *First*, I knew how eager Grandma was to improve
her communication skills. *Now* she can stay in touch with
all her loved ones. It really meant a lot to her. *Second*, by
familiarizing herself with the magical world of the Internet,
Grandma can now explore activities that she's always wanted

to experience. Having the ability to access the web was very empowering to her, and I haven't seen her that excited about something in a very long time. That alone was worth the experience of helping her learn about computer technology.

幫助他人學習

就在最近，我祖母決定買一台電腦，那她就能認識網路。她不了解現代科技，所以她要求我幫助她設定系統並開始瀏覽網頁。首先，我讓她看看如何打開和使用桌面上的程式。然後我幫助她建立一個電子郵件的帳號。最後，我們下載一個視訊會議的程式，那她就能打電話給其他住在世界各地的家庭成員。總之，我付出了下午較佳的時光教導祖母認識網路。

這樣的經驗有值得，有幾個原因。首先，我知道祖母非常渴望增進她的溝通技巧。現在，他可以和她愛的人保持聯絡。這對她意義重大。第二，藉由讓她了解網路這神奇的世界，祖母現在能夠探索她一直想要經歷的活動。能夠接觸網路給了她自主權，而我很久沒看過她對一件事情那麼興奮過。單單那樣值得了經歷幫助她學習電腦科技。

* **get acquainted with** 認識　　**be familiar with** 熟悉
modern (ˈmɑdən) *adj.* 現代的　　technology (tɛkˈnɑlədʒɪ) *n.* 科技
set up 設定　　system (ˈsɪstəm) *n.* 系統
get started 開始使用　　surf (sɝf) *v.* 瀏覽
web (wɛb) *n.* 網路　　program (ˈprogræm) *n.* 程式
desktop (ˈdɛskˌtɑp) *n.* (電腦的) 桌面
account (əˈkaʊnt) *n.* 帳戶　　download (ˌdaʊnˈlod) *v.* 下載
video conferencing 視訊會議　　**all in all** 總而言之
rewarding (rɪˈwɔrdɪŋ) *adj.* 有意義的；值得的
a couple of 一些；幾個　　eager (ˈigə) *adj.* 渴望的
improve (ɪmˈpruv) *v.* 增進
communication (kəˌmjunəˈkeʃən) *n.* 溝通

skill〔skɪl〕*n.* 技術;技能   ***stay in touch with*** 和…保持聯絡
mean a lot to sb. 對某人很重要;對某人意義重大
familiarize〔fəˋmɪljə͵raɪz〕*v.* 使熟悉
familiarize sb. with … 使某人熟悉…
magical〔ˋmædʒɪkl̩〕*adj.* 神奇的;不可思議的
explore〔ɪkˋsplor〕*v.* 探索   activity〔ækˋtɪvətɪ〕*n.* 活動
experience〔ɪkˋspɪrɪəns〕*v.* 體驗   ability〔əˋbɪlətɪ〕*n.* 能力
access〔ˋæksɛs〕*v.* 接觸;取得;利用
empowering〔ɪmˋpaʊrɪŋ〕*adj.* 給予自主權的
alone〔əˋlon〕*adv.* 單單;只有   worth〔wɝθ〕*adj.* 值得…的

📝103年指考作文範例

下圖呈現的是美國某高中的全體學生每天進行各種活動的時間分配,請寫一篇至少120個單詞的英文作文。文分兩段,第一段描述該圖所呈現之特別現象;第二段請說明整體而言,你一天的時間分配與該高中全體學生的異同,並說明其理由。

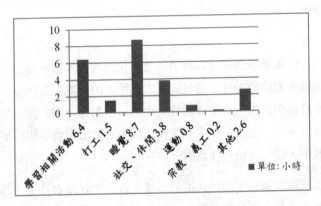

Perhaps *the most outstanding feature* of the chart is that these American students spend more time sleeping than anything else. *The second and third most special features* of the chart show that these students have part-time jobs and, apparently, busy social lives. This may seem unusual to non-American high school students. *Meanwhile*, it is also remarkable that the students spend two and a half hours a day doing something which is not clearly defined ("Other").

I think I spend my days in a very different way. *First of all*, I don't have a part-time job, practice a religion, volunteer for a cause, or exercise very often. *Second*, I rarely if ever have time for leisure activities. *As a result*, I spend much more time—about 12 hours a day—in learning-related activities. *That is to say*, I'm either in school, studying or sleeping. *Therefore*, my chart would look considerably different.

或許這張圖表最顯著的特色就是，比起其他事情，這些美國學生花比較多的時間睡覺。這張圖第二和第三的特點是這些學生有打工，而且很明顯的，有忙碌的社交生活。這對非美國的高中生顯得很不尋常。另一方面，學生一天花二個半小時做定義不明的事情（其他），這也是值得注意的。

我認為我過日子的方式很不一樣。首先，我沒有打工、信教、自願從事活動，或是常常運動。第二，我很少有時間做休閒活動。因此，我花很多時間——大約一天 12 小時——在學習相關的活動上。也就是說，我不是在學校讀書，就是睡覺。因此，我的圖表會看起來很不一樣。

* outstanding〔ˋaʊtˋstændɪŋ〕*adj.* 顯著的；突出的
feature〔ˋfitʃɚ〕*n.* 特徵；特色　　chart〔tʃɑrt〕*n.* 圖表
part-time *adj.* 兼職的；打工的
apparently〔əˋpærəntlɪ〕*adv.* 明顯地　　***social life*** 社交生活
non-（字首）非…　　meanwhile〔ˋmin,hwaɪl〕*adv.* 同時；另一方面
remarkable〔rɪˋmɑrkəbl〕*adj.* 值得注意的
define〔dɪˋfaɪn〕*v.* 定義　　practice〔ˋpræktɪs〕*v.* 實施；遵守
religion〔rɪˋlɪdʒən〕*n.* 宗教　　volunteer〔,vɑlənˋtɪr〕*v.* 志願從事
cause〔kɔz〕*n.* 目的；主張
rarely〔ˋrɛrlɪ〕*adv.* 很少地　　***rarely if ever*** 即使…也很少
leisure〔ˋliʒɚ〕*adj.* 空閒的；閒暇的　　***as a result*** 因此
that is to say 也就是說；換言之（= *in other words* = *namely*）
considerably〔kənˋsɪdərəblɪ〕*adv.* 頗；相當地

102年指考作文範例

提示： 以下有兩項即將上市之新科技產品：

> 產品一：隱形披風
> （invisibility cloak）
> 穿上後頓時隱形，旁人看不到你的存在；同時，隱形披風會保護你，讓你水火不侵。

> 產品二：智慧型眼鏡
> （smart glasses）
> 具有掃瞄透視功能，戴上後即能看到障礙物後方的生物；同時能完整紀錄你所經歷過的場景。

　　如果你有機會獲贈其中一項產品，你會選擇哪一項？請以此為主題，寫一篇至少 120 個單詞的英文作文。文分兩段，第一段說明你的選擇及理由，並舉例說明你將如何使用這項產品。第二段說明你不選擇另一項產品的理由及該項產品可能衍生的問題。

　　If I were lucky enough to win either prize, I would definitely prefer the smart glasses. ***First of all***, I think I could put them to better use than the invisibility cloak. ***For instance***, with the smart glasses, I could potentially use them to help people. If someone had an injury, I could identify the problem and possibly give them assistance before they could reach a hospital. Another benefit of the glasses would be the recording feature. *For example*, if I witnessed a traffic accident, I could provide the recording to the police so they could take appropriate action.

The invisibility cloak is not without its merits, but I think it would be used for more negative things like sneaking around or spying on people. Although the idea of being invisible is attractive, I personally can't think of a positive use for it. *Even worse*, if such a thing existed, it would almost certainly fall into the wrong hands. People would go around robbing banks and committing other crimes, and worst of all, get away with it. *So in conclusion*, I would prefer the prize that did the most good for society in general.

如果我夠幸運獲得其中一個獎品，我一定會比較喜歡智慧型眼鏡。首先，我認爲比起隱形斗蓬，我更可以善用它們。舉例來說，有智慧型眼鏡，我可以用它們去幫助人們。如果有人受傷，我可以辨識出問題，並可能在他們到達醫院前給予幫助。眼鏡的另一個好處是有自動記錄裝置的特點。舉例來說，如果我目擊一場交通意外，我可以提供該記錄給警方，如此他們便能夠採取適當的行動。

隱形斗蓬並不是沒有好處，但是我認爲它可能會用在比較負面的事情，像是偷偷摸摸地潛藏各處，或是偷窺他人。雖然無法被看見這點子很吸引人，我個人想不到它正面的用處。如果這樣的東西存在，它可能幾乎會落在壞人的手上。人們可能到處搶劫銀行，並犯下其他的罪行，而且最糟糕的是，逃脫罪刑。所以，總而言之，我偏好對社會整體來說有最大好處的獎品。

* prize〔praɪz〕*n.* 獎；獎品

definitely〔'dɛfənɪtlɪ〕*adv.* 明確地；一定

prefer〔prɪ'fɜ〕*v.* 較喜歡；偏好　　***first of all*** 首先

put…to use 使用　invisibility〔ɪn,vɪzə'bɪlətɪ〕*n.* 看不見；隱形

cloak〔klok〕*n.* 斗篷　　***for instance*** 舉例來說（= *for example*）

potentially〔pə'tɛnʃəlɪ〕*adv.* 可能地　injury〔'ɪndʒərɪ〕*n.* 受傷

identify〔aɪ'dɛntə,faɪ〕*v.* 辨識；看出

assistance〔ə'sɪstəns〕*n.* 幫助

meanwhile〔'min,hwaɪl〕*adv.* 同時　benefit〔'bɛnəfɪt〕*n.* 好處

recording〔rɪ'kɔrdɪŋ〕*adj.* 記錄的；自動記錄裝置的

feature〔'fitʃɚ〕*n.* 特色　witness〔'wɪtnɪs〕*v.* 目擊

appropriate〔ə'proprɪɪt〕*adj.* 適當的　action〔'ækʃən〕*n.* 行動

merit〔'mɛrɪt〕*n.* 好處；優點　negative〔'nɛgətɪv〕*adj.* 負面的

sneak〔snik〕*v.* 偷偷摸摸；鬼鬼祟祟　***spy on*** 暗中監視；偷窺

invisible〔ɪn'vɪzəbḷ〕*adj.* 看不見的；隱形的

personally〔'pɝsṇlɪ〕*adv.* 對個人而言　***think of*** 想到

positive〔'pɑzətɪv〕*adj.* 正面的　exist〔ɪg'zɪst〕*v.* 存在

fall into the wrong hands 落入不當的人手中；被不當使用

rob〔rɑb〕*v.* 搶劫　***commit crimes*** 犯罪

worst of all 最糟的是　***get away with***… 做…而未受懲罰

in conclusion 總而言之　***in general*** 一般來說；大體上

📝 101年指考作文範例

提示： 請以運動為主題，寫一篇至少 120 個單詞的文章，說明你最常從
　　　事的運動是什麼。文分兩段，第一段描述這項運動如何進行（如
　　　地點、活動方式、及可能需要的相關用品等），第二段說明你從
　　　事這項運動的原因及這項運動對你生活的影響。

　　Surfing is my favorite sport. Surfing of course takes

place on the ocean. ***First***, you get a surfboard and maybe a

wet suit (if the water is cold). ***Then*** you paddle out past the point where the waves come crashing in, which is called "the break." There you can observe the patterns of the waves and decide which one to take. Once you decide to take a wave, you must time your paddle strokes to catch the wave. If you catch the wave properly, then you try to stand up. This is the most difficult part of surfing.

Surfing is enjoyable to me for several reasons. *Mainly*, I enjoy being in the water. Surfing combines swimming with the sensation of riding down a ski slope. *In addition to* being intensely physical, surfing is also a calming activity. When you are out on the ocean, just you and your board, all the troubles in your life seem small and meaningless. You are humbled by the power and size of the ocean. *Therefore*, surfing is good for your mind and body.

衝浪是我最喜歡的運動。衝浪當然是發生在海洋。首先,你要有一個衝浪板,或許一件潛水衣(如果水很冷的話)。然後你划過海浪衝進的地方,叫做破浪點。在那裡你可以觀察到海浪的型態,並決定你要衝哪道浪。一定你決定要衝一道浪,你一定要計算你划動去抓浪的時間。如果你適時抓到了浪,然後你試著站立。這是衝浪最難的部分。

衝浪讓我感到非常愉快,有幾個原因。主要的原因是我喜歡在水裡面。衝浪結合了游泳和滑下雪坡的感受。除了需要非常激烈的體能,衝浪也是讓人冷靜的活動。當你在海洋上,只有你和你的衝浪板,你生命所有的煩惱都看似渺小沒有意義。你在海洋的廣大和魄力下感到謙卑。因此,衝浪對你的身心都有益處。

* surfing〔'sɜfɪŋ〕*n.* 衝浪　　***take place*** 發生；舉行
surfboard〔'sɜf͵bord〕*n.* 衝浪板　　***wet suit*** 潛水衣
paddle〔'pædl̩〕*v.* 划槳行進　　point〔pɔɪnt〕*n.* (空間的)某一點
wave〔wev〕*n.* 波浪　　crash〔kræʃ〕*v.* 撞擊
break〔brek〕*n.* 破浪點　　observe〔əb'zɜv〕*v.* 觀察
pattern〔'pætɚn〕*n.* 型態　　time〔taɪm〕*v.* 計算時間配合
stroke〔strok〕*n.* 一划　　properly〔'prɑpɚlɪ〕*adv.* 適當地；正確地
enjoyable〔ɪn'dʒɔɪəbl̩〕*adj.* 愉快的　　combine〔kəm'baɪn〕*v.* 結合
sensation〔sɛn'seʃən〕*n.* 感覺　　slope〔slop〕*n.* 斜坡
in addition to 除了…(還有)　　intensely〔ɪn'tɛnslɪ〕*adv.* 強烈地
physical〔'fɪzɪkl̩〕*adj.* 身體上的
meaningless〔'minɪŋlɪs〕*adj.* 無意義的
humble〔'hʌmbl̩〕*v.* 使變謙虛

✎ 100年指考作文範例

提示：　你認為畢業典禮應該是個溫馨感人、活潑熱鬧、或是嚴肅傷感的場景？請寫一篇英文作文說明你對畢業典禮的看法，第一段寫出畢業典禮對你而言意義是什麼，第二段說明要如何安排或進行活動才能呈現出這個意義。

A graduation ceremony is an event that celebrates an accomplishment. ***Indeed***, you have spent a number of years working toward a singular goal: a diploma. With that diploma, you can take the next step in your education, or perhaps, seek employment. Though the ceremony indicates a type of closure, that is, the end of one period of your life, it marks the beginning of another. ***Therefore***, while there may be some sadness in saying goodbye to old friends, it is quickly erased by the excitement of moving forward. No matter which grade level you graduate from, the moment marks the beginning of greater personal independence.

Following the ceremony, we should have a big party and invite our friends, family and former teachers to share the achievement. There should be food and drinks, music and dancing, and everybody should be encouraged to enjoy themselves. *What's more*, there shouldn't be any speeches or presentations. *Altogether*, the party should carry the spirit of excitement and celebrate the fact that we are taking the next step forward in the journey of life.

畢業典禮是慶祝成就的事件。的確，你花了幾年爲了一個目標而努力：文憑。有了那個文憑，你可以邁入你教育的下一步，或者可能是找工作。雖然畢業典禮表示某種結束，也就是你生命中一個階段的告結，這也代表了另一個階段的開始。因此，雖然對老朋友告別可能有點感傷，往前邁進的興奮感很快就能抹去悲傷。無論你從哪個層級畢業，該時刻代表著更多個人獨立的開始。

在畢業典禮之後，我們應該辦個盛大的派對，並邀請我們的朋友、家人，以及以前的老師來分享成就。應該要有食物和飲料、音樂，以及舞蹈，而且每個人應該被鼓勵要玩得盡興。此外，不該有任何的演講或報告。總之，該派對應該帶有興奮的精神，並慶祝我們正要往人生旅程的下一步邁進。

---

* celebrate ('sɛlə,bret) v. 慶祝
accomplishment (ə'kɑmplɪʃmənt) n. 成就
singular ('sɪŋgjələ) adj. 單一的　　diploma (dɪ'plomə) n. 文憑
seek (sik) v. 尋找　　employment (ɪm'plɔɪmənt) n. 就業
indicate ('ɪndə,ket) v. 表示　　closure ('kloʒə) n. 終止

that is 也就是說   mark〔mɑrk〕*v.* 標記   erase〔ɪ'res〕*v.* 拭去
former〔'fɔrmɚ〕*adj.* 先前的   *enjoy* oneself 玩得愉快
speech〔spitʃ〕*n.* 演講   presentation〔ˌprɛznʹteʃən〕*n.* 報告
spirit〔'spɪrɪt〕*n.* 精神   journey〔'dʒʒnɪ〕*n.* 旅程

✍99年指考作文範例

提示： 在你的記憶中，哪一種氣味（smell）最讓你難忘？請寫一篇英文
作文，文長至少120字，文分兩段，第一段描述你在何種情境中
聞到這種氣味，以及你初聞這種氣味時的感受，第二段描述這個
氣味至今仍令你難忘的理由。

An Unforgettable Smell

The sense of smell is one of the most important attributes
in life. *In fact*, many of our precious memories are shaped by the
scents attached to them. *Personally*, the most unforgettable
smell is the aroma of my grandmother's cooking. When I was
young, I especially looked forward to visiting my grandmother's
place during holidays. Whenever we stopped by, she always
cooked my favorite chicken soup. I can still remember the cozy
feeling that embraced me when I first smelled it. *Simply put*, the
warmth and gratification it brought me was simply
indescribable.

Growing up in a single-parent family, I saw home-cooked
food as a luxury. Since my mother worked two jobs, we always
ate separately. Eating alone on a regular basis, I felt lonely and
isolated from time to time. *Luckily*, grandmother's chicken soup
reminded me that I still belonged to a family. Through smelling

UNIT 9

and tasting her soup, I felt loved and treasured again. Although she is no longer with us, the memory of her fragrant chicken soup will stay with me for the rest of my life. ***Most importantly***, it will surely serve as the reminder of how lucky I was.

難忘的氣味

　　氣味是生命中最重要的特質之一。事實上,許多我們過往的記憶是由附帶的味道所塑造的。對我來說,最難忘的味道是我祖母烹飪的香味。當我年幼的時候,我特別期待假日的時候拜訪我祖母。每當我順道拜訪的時候,她總是煮我最喜歡的雞湯。我依然記得,當我第一次聞到該味道,那環繞著我舒服的感受。簡而言之,它帶給我溫暖和滿足,是難以言喻的。

　　在單親家庭長大,我視家常菜為奢侈品。因為我母親做兩份工作,我們總是各自吃飯。常常獨自吃飯,我偶爾感到孤獨無依。幸運的是,祖母的雞湯讓我想起我依然還是屬於家庭的一部份。透過嗅聞和品嚐她的湯,我再次感到被愛和珍惜。雖然她不再和我們一起了,記憶中她充滿香味的雞湯依然伴隨著我的接下來的人生。最重要的是,這確定能提醒著我有多幸運。

---

* attribute〔'ætrə‚bjut〕*n.* 特質　　precious〔'prɛʃəs〕*adj.* 寶貴的
shape〔ʃep〕*v.* 塑造　　scent〔sɛnt〕*n.* 氣味
be attached to 附屬於　　unforgettable〔‚ʌnfɚ'gɛtəbḷ〕*adj.* 難忘的
aroma〔ə'romə〕*n.* 香味　　cozy〔'kozɪ〕*adj.* 舒適愜意的
embrace〔ɪm'bres〕*v.* 環繞　　gratification〔‚grætəfə'keʃən〕*n.* 滿足
indescribable〔‚ɪndɪ'skraɪbəbḷ〕*adj.* 難以形容的
single-parent *adj.* 單親的　　luxury〔'lʌkʃərɪ〕*n.* 奢侈品
separately〔'sɛpərɪtlɪ〕*adv.* 個別地
on a regular basis 經常地 (= *regularly*)
isolated〔'aɪsḷ‚etɪd〕*adj.* (被) 孤立的
fragrant〔'fregrənt〕*adj.* 芳香的　　***serve as*** 充當;當作
reminder〔rɪ'maɪndɚ〕*n.* 提醒物

✒️98年指考作文範例

提示：如果你可以不用擔心預算，隨心所欲的度過一天，你會怎麼過？
　　　請寫一篇短文，第一段說明你會邀請誰和你一起度過這一天？為
　　　什麼？第二段描述你會去哪裡？做些什麼事？為什麼？

A Day Without a Budget

My family isn't poor, but we aren't exactly rich, either.
However, my parents still give the best of everything to me and
my siblings. *Therefore*, if there comes a day when money is
not an issue, I'll definitely treat my family. No one has given
me more than they have, so they deserve it. *For this reason*, I
have made special plans for every member of my family, and I
just know they're going to love them.

First of all, my plans include taking my mom and my
sister to the mall for some shopping. They can finally get the
new dresses and shoes they've wanted. *Then*, for my dad, I'll
bring him to the auto shop and give his car the best upgrade and
maintenance there is. We can even paint it red, as it's what
he's always wanted. *Meanwhile*, for my brother, I'll take him
to a pro basketball game, and get his favorite player to talk to
him and sign autographs for him. He's probably going to faint.
Finally, when they're all done and satisfied, I'll have seats
ready for them at the best steak house in town, where we can
enjoy some quality family time. What will I get? I will get to
see my family laugh and smile.

UNIT 9

沒有預算的一天

　　我的家庭並不窮，但是我們也不富有。不過，我的父母依然把最好的東西給我和我的兄弟姊妹。因此，如果有一天，錢不是問題的話，我一定會請我的家人。沒有人給我的比他們還多，所以他們應得這樣的待遇。因此，我已經做了特別的計畫，給我各個家庭成員，而且我知道他們會喜歡的。

　　首先，我的計畫包含帶我母親和妹妹去賣場購物。她們最後可以買到她們一直想要的洋裝和鞋子。然後，至於我父親，我會帶他到汽車工廠，讓他的車享有最好的升級和保養。我們甚至會把車子漆成紅色，因為這是他一直想要的。同時，我弟弟的話，我會帶他去看職業籃球賽，並讓他最喜歡的球員和他講話並給他簽名照。他可能會就要暈倒了。最後，當他們都完成這些而滿足了，我會準備好座位，在鎮上最好的牛排館，享受美好的家庭時間。我能得到什麼呢？我將能夠看到我的家人堆滿笑容。

---

* budget〔ˋbʌdʒɪt〕*n.* 預算　　siblings〔ˋsɪblɪŋs〕*n. pl.* 兄弟姊妹
issue〔ˋɪʃjʊ〕*n.* 問題　　definitely〔ˋdɛfənɪtlɪ〕*adv.* 一定
auto〔ˋɔto〕*n.*【口語】汽車　　　***auto shop*** 汽車工廠
upgrade〔ˋʌpˏgred〕*n.* 升級
maintenance〔ˋmentənəns〕*n.* 維修；保養
pro〔pro〕*adj.* 職業的（= *professional*）
autograph〔ˋɔtəˏgræf〕*n.* 親筆簽名　　faint〔fent〕*v.* 暈倒
done〔dʌn〕*adj.* 完成的；結束的　　***steak house*** 牛排餐廳
quality〔ˋkwɑlətɪ〕*adj.* 優質的（= *excellent*）　　***get to V.*** 得以；能夠

📝 97年指考作文範例

提示：　廣告在我們生活中隨處可見。請寫一篇大約 120-150 字的短文，介紹一則令你印象深刻的電視或平面廣告。第一段描述該廣告的內容（如：主題、故事情節、音樂、畫面等），第二段說明該廣告令你印象深刻的原因。

【範例 1】

An Impressive Commercial

One of the commercials that I remember the most is one for Regaine, a medicine for use against hair loss. Pictures of a middle-aged man are shown from left to right, each one with less hair than the one before it. The man looks more and more depressed. *However*, the last picture shows the Regaine product, and the pictures now go from right to left, with the man smiling happily at the end.

I am impressed by this commercial because it looks realistic. Most hair growth product commercials show a bald man. *Then after* using the product, he "magically" grows hair again. *However*, this commercial shows the entire process of losing hair, and the gradual re-growth after using Regaine. I think it's more convincing than other hair-growth commercials, so I think it's quite impressive.

一則印象深刻的廣告

　　我記憶最深的一個廣告是落建，一個治療掉髮的藥。照片由左向右顯示一位中年男子，每一張照片都比前一張的頭髮還要少。男子看起來越來越沮喪。不過，最後一張照片顯示落建這產品，而這些照片由右到左，男子最後開心地笑了。

　　我對這廣告印象深刻，因為這看起來很真實。很多毛髮生長的產品廣告顯示一位禿頭男子。然後在使用該產品後，他「神奇地」又長出了頭髮。不過，這則廣告顯示了全部落髮的過程，以及在使用落建後逐漸重新生髮。我覺得這比其他生髮的廣告來得有說服力，所以我覺得相當難忘。

【範例2】

An Impressive Commercial

During the recent NBA playoffs, the NBA released a series of player commercials. The commercials showed two players from competing teams, with each showing just one half of his or her face. The two faces were pieced together, and the players spoke the same lines, so it looked like one face with one voice. *All in all*, a total of 15 commercials were made.

These commercials were impressive because they showed how much the players wanted to win. *Accordingly*, the lines were all very dramatic and emotional, and it was easy to believe that the players meant it from the heart. No matter who you are playing against, you give your all for the chance to win. *In closing*, I was moved by many of these commercials, and that's why I remember them so well.

一則印象深刻的廣告

在最近的NBA季後賽，NBA發行了一系列的廣告。廣告出現兩位來自競爭隊伍的球員，彼此只有露出他或她一半的臉。兩個臉拼接在一起，而且球員們講一樣的台詞，所以這看起來像是一張臉一個聲音。總的來說，共製作了15個廣告。

　　這些廣告讓人印象深刻，因爲它們表現了球員多麼想要贏得勝利。因此，台詞都非常激情且感動人心，很容易就相信球員們他們是說出內心話。無論你是在對抗誰，你要出百分之百的力量才有機會贏。總之，裡面許多廣告感動著我，而那就是爲何我依然記得它們。

* **hair loss** 掉髮　　**middle-age** 中年
depressed〔dɪˈprɛst〕*adj.* 沮喪的　　realistic〔ˌriəˈlɪstɪk〕*adj.* 現實的
bald〔bɔld〕*adj.* 禿頭的　　magically〔ˈmædʒɪklɪ〕*adv.* 不可思議地
gradual〔ˈgrædʒʊəl〕*adj.* 逐漸的　　growth〔groθ〕*n.* 生長
NBA 國家籃球協會（= *National Basketball Association*）
playoffs〔ˈpleˌɔf〕*n.* 季後賽　　release〔rɪˈlis〕*v.* 發行；發表
series〔ˈsɪrɪz〕*n.* 系列　　compete〔kəmˈpit〕*v.* 競爭
one half 一半　　piece〔pis〕*v.* 拼合
line〔laɪn〕*n.* 臺詞　　dramatic〔drəˈmætɪk〕*adj.* 充滿激情的
emotional〔ɪˈmoʃənḷ〕*adj.* 激起情感的　　**mean it** 認眞的
from the heart 發自內心；眞誠地（= *sincerely*）
give your all 出百分之百的力量　　move〔muv〕*v.* 感動

UNIT 9

📝96年指考作文範例

提示：你能想像一個沒有電（electricity）的世界嗎？請寫一篇文章，第一段描述我們的世界沒有了電以後，會是甚麼樣子，第二段說明這樣的世界是好是壞，並舉例解釋原因。

【範例 1】

A World Without Electricity

　　A world without electricity would spell the end for many people. *For one thing*, most forms of communication and transportation we rely so much on would be cut off. *For another*, International trade would be down for good, and the whole world would be affected. Most of us wouldn't even know how to live anymore.

A worldwide power failure would be a disaster—and a blessing in disguise. No electricity means no modern conveniences, and the source of provisions would be a problem, not to mention the riots that would break out. *On the other hand*, Mother Earth has suffered greatly because of technological advances, and such a power outage would certainly stop the damage. It all comes down to what we care about more—the world we live *in*, or the world we live *on*?

沒有電的世界

　　一個沒有電的世界對很多人來說意味著終結。其一，我們非常仰賴的溝通方式和交通大多都被切斷。其二，國際貿易會永久停擺，而且整個世界都會受到影響。大多數的我們甚至不知道要如何過活。

　　全世界都斷電會是個大災難——也是因禍得福。沒有電代表著沒有現代的便利設施，而且糧食的來源也會是個問題，更不用說會爆發的騷動。另一方面來說，因為科技的進步，大自然之母已經承受很大的傷害，而斷電確定能停止傷害。這全歸結到我們關心什麼比較多——我們生活的世界，還是我們所依存的世界。

【範例2】

A World Without Electricity

A world without electricity would be very different from the one we know today. We would no longer enjoy many conveniences such as computers, televisions, household appliances, or even lights at night. *In addition*, the productivity of many factories would be reduced. All kinds of goods would become scarce and expensive.　We would also lose the ability to communicate instantly with others.

　　In my opinion, the world would be worse off without electricity.　Although its production causes environmental pollution, we are too dependent on it to give it up.　Electricity affects nearly every aspect of modern-day life.　Without it, we would no longer enjoy any of the technological advances of the past century.　*For example*, we would have to give up refrigeration, satellite communications, and life-saving medical devices.　*In short*, electricity is simply too valuable to do without.

UNIT 9

沒有電的世界

　　一個沒有電的世界會和我們今日所認識的世界非常不一樣。我們不再能享有許多便利的設施，像是電腦、電視、家電，或者甚至晚上的燈光。此外，很多工廠的生產力會降低。所有的物品都會變得稀少且昂貴。我們也會失去和他人立即溝通的能力。

　　依我之見，沒有電，整個世界將會每況愈下。雖然生產會造成環境污染，我們過度依賴而無法放棄生產。電力幾乎現代生活的每個面向。沒有電，我們將不再能享有上個世紀任何科技的進步。我們將會必須放棄冰箱、衛星通訊，以及救命的醫療設施。簡而言之，電力實在太珍貴而不能缺少。

---

* spell〔spɛl〕*v.* 意味　　***cut off*** 中斷；切斷　　***for good*** 永久地
worldwide〔'wɜld,waɪd〕*adj.* 全球性的　　***power failure*** 斷電
blessing〔'blɛsɪŋ〕*n.* 恩賜　　disguise〔dɪs'gaɪz〕*n.* 假扮
blessing in disguise 因禍得福　　source〔sors〕*n.* 來源
provision〔prə'vɪʒən〕*n.* 糧食；必需品　　riot〔'raɪət〕*n.* 暴動；騷亂

break out 爆發；突然發生　　advance〔əd'væns〕v. 發展
outage〔'autɪdʒ〕n. (水、電等的) 中斷供應
come down to 歸結為　　household〔'haus,hold〕adj. 家用的
appliance〔ə'plaɪəns〕n. 器具；設備
household appliance 家用電器；家電產品
productivity〔,prodʌk'tɪvətɪ〕n. 生產力
scarce〔skɛrs〕adj. 稀有的；珍貴的
worse off 每況愈下的　　aspect〔'æspɛkt〕n. 方面
refrigeration〔rɪ,frɪdʒə'reʃən〕n. 冷藏；冷凍
satellite〔'sætḷ,aɪt〕n. 衛星

📝 95年指考作文範例

提示：　人的生活中，難免有遭人誤解因而感到委屈的時候。請以此為主
題，寫一篇至少 120 字的英文作文；第一段描述個人被誤解的經
驗，第二段談這段經驗對個人的影響與啟示。

On Being Misunderstood

It seems that no matter how hard we try, we are not
always understood. Misunderstandings can cause confusion
or mistakes. ***Sometimes*** they are funny, ***but sometimes*** they can
cause hurt feelings. This once happened to me.

Last year my teacher asked us to do some research and
make a presentation to our class. This was a difficult challenge
for me. ***In fact***, one of my classmates had the same problem. I
knew that she needed help, but I thought my advice would only
make her more confused and worried. I even said to one of
my friends that I hoped she wouldn't ask me for help.

Unfortunately, she heard about this. She misunderstood my meaning and thought I was too selfish to help her. She even refused to speak to me after this.

Luckily, I found out why my classmate was upset and I was able to talk to her about it. When she understood my reason for not helping her, she forgave me. From this experience I learned that the only way to resolve a misunderstanding is to communicate.

論誤解

看似無論我們多努力，我們無法總是被了解。誤解可能會造成困惑或錯誤。有時候它們很好笑，但是有時候它們會造成感情上的傷害。這曾經發生在我身上。

去年我的老師要求我們做些研究，並報告給班上的人聽。這對我來說是個困難的挑戰。事實上，我其中一位同班同學有一樣的問題。我知道她需要幫助，但我覺得我的建議只會讓她更困惑且更擔心。我甚至對我其中一位朋友說，我希望她不會向我求助。不幸的，她聽說了這件事。她誤解我的意思，而且認為我太自私而不願幫助她。她甚至之後拒絕跟我說話。

幸運地，我發現為何我的同班同學很沮喪，而我能夠跟她談談這件事。當她了解我不幫助她的原因後，她原諒了我。從這個經驗，我學到了唯一處理誤會的方式就是溝通。

* misunderstand (ˌmɪsʌndəˈstænd) v. 誤會
  no matter how 無論怎麼樣
  misunderstanding (ˌmɪsʌndəˈstændɪŋ) n. 誤會
  confusion (kənˈfjuʒən) n. 困惑

mistake〔məˋstek〕*n.* 錯誤；誤會　　hurt〔hɜt〕*adj.* 受傷的
once〔wʌns〕*adv.* 曾經　　research〔rɪˋsɝtʃ〕*n.* 研究
presentation〔͵prɛznˋteʃən〕*n.* 發表；描述
difficult〔ˋdɪfə͵kʌlt〕*adj.* 困難的　　challenge〔ˋtʃælɪndʒ〕*n.* 挑戰
advice〔ədˋvaɪs〕*n.* 建議　　confused〔kənˋfjuzd〕*adj.* 困惑的
unfortunately〔ʌnˋfɔrtʃənɪtlɪ〕*adv.* 不幸地
meaning〔ˋminɪŋ〕*n.* 意思　　selfish〔ˋsɛlfɪʃ〕*adj.* 自私的
refuse〔rɪˋfjuz〕*v.* 拒絕　　forgive〔fəˋgɪv〕*v.* 原諒
experience〔ɪkˋspɪrɪəns〕*n.* 經驗　　resolve〔rɪˋzɑlv〕*v.* 解決
communicate〔kəˋmjunə͵ket〕*v.* 溝通

✍ 94年指考作文範例

提示：　指定科目考試完畢後，高中同學決定召開畢業後的第一次同學會，
　　　　你被公推負責主辦。請將你打算籌辦的活動寫成一篇短文。文分
　　　　兩段，第一段詳細介紹同學會的時間、地點及活動內容，第二段
　　　　則說明採取這種活動方式的理由。

An Activity for Graduates

Now that the Joint College Entrance Exam is over, we
are about to begin a brand-new and exciting stage in our
lives. *However*, it is important to remember the past and
keep in touch with those who have made our high school
years special. *Therefore*, we have organized a picnic for all
the graduates. *In addition to* a barbecue, there will be games
and a singing contest. The event will take place on Sunday,
July 17, at Yangmingshan Park. Buses will leave the school
at 11:00 am and return at 5:00 pm.

I hope that all of our graduates will attend, for this may be our last chance to spend some time together. During the activity we may share our memories of high school and our plans for the future. *Most importantly*, it is a chance for us to end our high school careers on a positive note by relaxing and having fun after enduring the stress of the JCEE.

畢業生活動

現在聯考已經結束了，我們正要開始一段人生中嶄新又刺激的階段。然而，要記得過去並和那些使我們高中歲月特別的人保持聯絡，這是很重要的。因此，我們安排了野餐給所有畢業生。除了烤肉，會有遊戲和唱歌比賽。活動會在7月17日，星期日舉辦，地點是陽明山公園。公車會在早上11點停在學校，下午5點回來。

我希望所有的畢業生都會參加，因為這可能是我們最後一次機會聚在一起。在這個活動中，我們可能分享高中的記憶，以及未來的計畫。最重要的是，在承受聯考的壓力後，藉由放鬆和盡情玩樂，這是個以樂觀的氣氛結束我們高中生涯的機會。

* graduate ('grædʒuɪt) *n.* 畢業生　　*now that* 現在；既然
Joint College Extrance Exam 聯合大學入學考試
be about to V. 正要～；即將～　　brand-new *adj.* 全新的
stage (stedʒ) *n.* 舞台；階段　　*keep in touch* 保持聯絡
organize ('ɔrgən‚aɪz) *v.* 組織；安排　　picnic ('pɪknɪk) *n.* 野餐
in addition to 除了…（還有）　　barbecue ('bɑrbɪ‚kju) *n.* 烤肉
contest ('kɑntɛst) *n.* 比賽　　*take place* 舉辦；發生
attend (ə'tɛnd) *v.* 出席；參加
most importantly 最重要的是（= *above all*）
career (kə'rɪr) *n.* 生涯；經歷
positive ('pɑzətɪv) *adj.* 正面的；樂觀的　　note (not) *n.* 氣氛；感受
on a positive note 用樂觀的角度；樂觀地　　*have fun* 玩得愉快
endure (ɪn'dur) *v.* 忍耐；承受　　stress (strɛs) *n.* 壓力

📝 93年指考作文範例

提示： 請以 "Travel Is the Best Teacher" 爲主題，寫一篇至少 120 個字
的英文作文。第一段針對文章主題，說明旅行的優點，並在第二
段舉自己在國內或國外的旅行經驗，以印證第一段的說明。

Travel Is the Best Teacher

I believe that travel is the best teacher. There are so many things you can learn from traveling that you may never experience in a classroom or from a book. *Generally speaking*, traveling broadens your horizons. It lets you meet new people and helps you experience things in person instead of reading about them.

For instance, I remember when I went to Greece for the first time. I saw the ancient ruins of the Parthenon and the Acropolis. *Of course*, they are amazing sights to behold. You can feel the history vibrating from these buildings when you first lay eyes on them. *Moreover*, I also learned about Greek food and culture just by walking around the streets. *Another* good thing about traveling is the people you get to meet. *To my delight*, I met many travelers in my hostel and we exchanged amazing stories that I still remember to this day.

These are things that you may read about in books or learn from teachers. *But* unless you experience them in person, you are just going to forget within a few years. *Overall*, traveling has left a lasting impression on me, a feat not many of my teachers can claim to have accomplished.

旅行是最好的老師

　　我相信旅行是最好的老師。從旅行中你可以學到很多東西，這些是你在教室或是書本裡可能從未體驗的。通常，旅行拓展你的視野。它讓你認識新的人，並幫助你親自體驗事物，而非只是閱讀。

　　舉例來說，我記得當我第一次去希臘的時候。我看到巴特農神殿的遺跡和衛城。當然，它們是驚人的景觀。當你第一次看到它們，你可以感受到歷史從這些建築物中顫動出來。此外，只靠著在街道上到處走動，我也學習到了關於希臘的食物和文化。另一個旅行的好處是你可以認識的人們。很高興的是，我在青年旅社遇到很多旅客，而且我們交流了很驚奇的故事，這些我到今天依然記得。

　　這些事物你可能在書本上或是從老師身上得知。但是除非你自己去體驗，你可能幾年的時間就會忘記。整體而言，旅行留給了我一個深刻的感受，這功績不是我很多的老師聲稱可以達成的。

UNIT 9

＊ experience〔ɪkˋspɪrɪəns〕v. 經歷；體驗　　broaden〔ˋbrɔdn̩〕v. 增廣
horizons〔həˋraɪznz〕n. pl.（知識、經驗等的）範圍
***broaden** one's **horizons** 使某人增廣見聞　　in person 親自*
***instead of** 而不是　　Greece〔gris〕n. 希臘*
ancient〔ˋænʃənt〕adj. 古代的　　ruins〔ˋruɪnz〕n. pl. 廢墟；遺跡
Parthenon〔ˋparθə͵nan〕n. 巴特農神殿（在希臘雅典衛城山崗上，
*　爲雅典娜女神的神殿）*
Acropolis〔əˋkrapəlɪs〕n.（雅典的）衛城
amazing〔əˋmezɪŋ〕adj. 令人驚奇的
sights〔saɪts〕n. pl. 觀光名勝　　behold〔bɪˋhold〕v. 看
vibrate〔ˋvaɪbret〕v. 震動
***lay eye on**（第一次）看到（= set eyes on）*
***get to** + V. 有機會去…　　hostel〔ˋhastl̩〕n. 青年旅舍*
exchange〔ɪksˋtʃendʒ〕v. 交換　　to this day 至今
lasting〔ˋlæstɪŋ〕adj. 持久的；永恆的
impression〔ɪmˋprɛʃən〕n. 印象 < on >　　feat〔fit〕n. 功績
claim〔klem〕v. 自稱　　accomplish〔əˋkamplɪʃ〕v. 達成

✍ 92年指考作文範例

提示： 小考、段考、複習考、畢業考、甚至校外其它各種大大小小的考
試，已成爲高中學生生活中不可或缺的一部份。請寫一篇 120 至
150 個單詞左右的英文作文，文分兩段，第一段以 Exams of all
kinds have become a necessary part of my high school life. 爲
主題句；第二段則以 The most unforgettable exam I have ever
taken is... 爲開頭並加以發展。

*Exams of all kinds have become a necessary part of my
high school life.* This is an unavoidable reality that I have
accepted. For the last year, I have been pressured and
challenged by daily quizzes, weekly tests and exams. I
sometimes feel like a test-taking machine. I'm not a big fan
of exams; *however*, I realize they are an indispensable tool in
measuring performance, knowledge and progress. I know
exams are a positive challenge to help me improve. *Therefore*,
I must face exams with courage and confidence.

The most unforgettable exam I have ever taken is the exam
I'm taking right now! This College Entrance Exam is the
most important exam of my life. The results will determine
my future education and career path. The pressure is intense.
My family's expectations are very high! I am praying for a
high score! *So* here I sit, struggling and sweating over this
composition. *Of course* this exam is the most unforgettable
one!

　　各種考試已經成為我高中生活一個必要的部分。這是無法避免的事實，我已經接受。在過去的一年，我受到的壓力和挑戰，來自每天的小考、週考，和大考。我有時候覺得像是一個考試機器。我不是崇尚考試的人；不過，我了解它們是測量表現、知識，和進步的一個不可或缺的工具。我知道考試是正面的挑戰來幫助我進步。因此，我必須勇敢且有自信地面對考試。

　　我考過最難忘的考試是我目前的考試！這大學入學考試是我一生中最重要的考試。成績結果會決定我未來的教育和職業生涯。壓力很大。我家人的期望很高！我期待得高分！所以，我坐在這裡掙扎，並為了這作文而奮鬥。當然這個考試是最難忘的一個！

UNIT 9

* unavoidable〔ˌʌnəˈvɔɪdəbl̩〕*adj.* 無法避免的
reality〔rɪˈælətɪ〕*n.* 事實　　pressure〔ˈprɛʃɚ〕*v.* 對～施加壓力
challenge〔ˈtʃælɪndʒ〕*v. n.* 挑戰　　daily〔ˈdelɪ〕*adj.* 每天的
quiz〔kwɪz〕*n.* 小考　　weekly〔ˈwiklɪ〕*adj.* 每週的
test-taking machine 考試機器　　realize〔ˈriəˌlaɪz〕*v.* 了解
indispensable〔ˌɪndɪˈspɛnsəbl̩〕*adj.* 不可或缺的
tool〔tul〕*n.* 工具　　measure〔ˈmɛʒɚ〕*v.* 衡量
performance〔pɚˈfɔrməns〕*n.* 表現
progress〔ˈprɑgrɛs〕*n.* 進步　　positive〔ˈpɑzətɪv〕*adj.* 正面的
confidence〔ˈkɑnfədəns〕*n.* 信心
unforgettable〔ˌʌnfɚˈgɛtəbl̩〕*adj.* 難忘的
college entrance exam 大學入學考試　　career〔kəˈrɪr〕*n.* 事業
path〔pæθ〕*n.* 方向　　intense〔ɪnˈtɛns〕*adj.* 強烈的
expectation〔ˌɛkspɛkˈteʃən〕*n.* 期望　　pray〔pre〕*v.* 祈禱
score〔skor〕*n.* 分數　　struggle〔ˈstrʌgl̩〕*v.* 掙扎；奮鬥
sweat〔swɛt〕*v.* 流汗；辛苦（工作）
composition〔ˌkɑmpəˈzɪʃən〕*n.* 作文

✎ 91年指考作文範例

提示： 文章請以 "If I won two million dollars in the lottery, I would help…" 開始，敘述如果你或妳贏得台灣樂透彩新台幣兩百萬元之後，最想把全數金額拿去幫助的人、機構或組織，並寫出理由。

If I won two million dollars in the lottery, *I would help* the homeless people I see every day loitering around the train station. *For one thing*, I don't know why those people are homeless, but I would bet there must be some sad stories there. *Honestly*, it doesn't matter what those people have done or failed at in the past; no person deserves to live like that. *However*, I would not walk up to them and blatantly offer them money because it would rob them of their dignity. I would help them subtly.

To do this, I would contact the city Social Welfare Department and inform them of my intention and request them to set up a program to help the homeless. *At the same time*, I would volunteer some of my time to supervise the spending of the money and the distribution of the goods purchased with the money. We could also use the money to start a job training and placement program. Although two million dollars is not a big sum by any means, I do believe that this trivial amount could make a difference for the homeless. *Ultimately*, if everyone can chip in a little every day, then pretty soon homelessness will become a thing of the past.

　　如果我樂透贏得兩百萬，我會幫助我每天看到在火車站遊蕩的街友。首先，我不知道爲何這些人無家可歸，但是我敢說一定有一些難過的故事。老實說，那些人在過去做了什麼，或是做什麼事失敗了，都不重要；沒有人理應那樣子過活。然而，我不會走到他們的面前，公然地給他們錢，因爲這會剝奪了他們的尊嚴。我會低調地幫助他們。

　　爲了做到這點，我會聯絡社會福利局，並通知他們我的意圖，並要求他們設立一個計畫來幫助街友。同時，我會自願挪出我的時間去監督錢的花費，以及該錢所購得物資的分配。我們也可以用該筆錢來開啓職業訓練和就業安置計畫。雖然兩百萬絕對不是一大筆錢，我深信這微不足道的金錢對街友可以有很大的差別。最後，如果每個人每天捐一點錢，那麼很快無家可歸的現象將成爲歷史。

UNIT 9

* loiter〔ˈlɔɪtɚ〕*v.* 閒混　　bet〔bɛt〕*v.* 打賭
deserve〔dɪˈzɝv〕*v.* 應得　　***walk up*** 走近
blatantly〔ˈblɛtn̩tlɪ〕*adv.* 公然地；突兀地　　rob〔rɑb〕*v.* 奪走
dignity〔ˈdɪgnətɪ〕*n.* 尊嚴　　subtly〔ˈsʌtlɪ〕*adv.* 低調地
Social Welfare Department 社會福利局
inform〔ɪnˈfɔrm〕*v.* 通知　　***set up*** 設立
program〔ˈprogræm〕*n.* 計劃　　volunteer〔ˌvɑlənˈtɪr〕*v.* 自願
supervise〔ˈsupɚˈvaɪz〕*v.* 監督；管理
distribution〔ˌdɪstrəˈbjuʃən〕*n.* 配給
placement〔ˈplesmənt〕*n.* 職業介紹
sum〔sʌm〕*n.* 總額；總數　　***by any means*** 無論如何
trivial〔ˈtrɪvɪəl〕*adj.* 微不足道的　　***chip in*** 捐款

如何寫英文作文練習解答

自我測驗 (P. 9)

1. pride goes before a fall → <u>Pride Goes Before a Fall</u>

2. why I want to attend college
   → <u>Why I Want to Attend College</u>

3. laughter is better than medicine
   → <u>Laughter Is Better than Medicine</u>

4. the person who influenced me most
   → <u>The Person Who Influenced Me Most</u>

5. eating in Taiwan → <u>Eating in Taiwan</u>

6. if I had magic power → <u>If I Had Magic Power</u>

7. helping others is the root of happiness
   → <u>Helping Others Is the Root of Happiness</u>

8. never put off till tomorrow what you can do today
   → <u>Never Put Off till Tomorrow What You Can Do Today</u>

9. knowledge is power → <u>Knowledge Is Power</u>

10. money isn't everything → <u>Money Isn't Everything</u>

11. health is better than wealth → <u>Health Is Better than Wealth</u>

12. what I want to do most after the college entrance exam
    → <u>What I Want to Do Most After the College Entrance Exam</u>

13. the country I want to visit most
    → <u>The Country I Want to Visit Most</u>

14. the most unforgettable experience
    → <u>The Most Unforgettable Experience</u>

15. city life and country life → <u>City Life and Country Life</u>

16. if I were an English teacher → <u>If I Were an English Teacher</u>

17. how to overcome your laziness
    → <u>How to Overcome Your Laziness</u>

18. don't give up halfway → <u>Don't Give Up Halfway</u>

19. a sense of humor → <u>A Sense of Humor</u>

20. honesty is the best policy → <u>Honesty Is the Best Policy</u>

文意選填：**Test 1**（P. 19）

1. C	2. E	3. I	4. D	5. B	6. G	7. K	8. F
9. H	10. A						

文意選填：**Test 2**（P. 20）

11. C	12. D	13. E	14. G	15. F	16. H	17. B	18. A
19. M	20. N						

參考解答（P. 23）

【例 1】　(B) These are reasons to see a doctor.

【例 2】　(B) These are three types of movie.

【例3】 (B) These are differences between city life and country life.

【例4】 (A) These are the leading causes of death.

【例5】 (D) These are causes of global warming.

【例6】 (C) These are reasons why people may exercise.

【例7】 (A) These are the steps in growing flowers.

【例8】 (C) These are the characteristics of a good doctor.

【例9】 (C) These are advantages of being a celebrity.

參考解答（P. 28）

【例1】 A graduation ceremony symbolizes an accomplishment.

【例2】 This is the most unforgettable exam I have ever taken.

【例3】 I believe that travel is the best teacher.

【例4】 Bullying has no place in our society.

【例5】 Life without electricity would be disastrous.

【例6】 We have organized a picnic for all the graduates.

【例7】 We cannot avoid being misunderstood.

【例8】 I cannot forget the commercial for hair-loss medicine.

【例9】 Smells can leave a lasting impression.

【例10】 TV has become a staple of modern life.

【例 11】 Everyone has experienced insomnia.

【例 12】 Laziness will lead people nowhere.

【例 13】 Honest people are appreciated by others.

【例 14】 We have to work together with others to exist in this world.

【例 15】 My mother is an ordinary housewife.

【例 16】 Sunday is an important day for my family.

【例 17】 Nothing is more powerful than money.

【例 18】 My motto is "Whatever is worth doing is worth doing well."

【例 19】 Taiwan's night markets are unique.

【例 20】 A sense of responsibility is perhaps the most important element in personal success.

解

答

參考解答（P. 30）

【例 1】 I have made several visits to New York.

【例 2】 Bob is a good basketball player.

【例 3】 There are thee steps involved in making a woodcut.

【例 4】 Doctors can now examine babies before they are born.

【例 5】 Bob did not look healthy at all.

【例 6 】 I love summer best of all seasons.

【例 7 】 It is our duty to be law-abiding citizens in our community.

【例 8 】 As the proverb says, "No man is an island."

【例 9 】 Books play an important part in our lives.

【例 10 】 It is important to exercise regularly.

歷屆考題觀摩：參考解答（P. 35）

【例 1 】 B / A

【例 2 】 B / A / D

【例 3 】 D / A / B

【例 4 】 A / C / D / B

【例 5 】 B / C / A

【例 6 】 B

【例 7 】 C / A / B

作文範例：參考解答（P. 45）

【例 1 】 是

【例 2 】 否

My brother quit the job because it was too dangerous.

【例 3 】 否

Spring recess was the best vacation I have ever had.

【例 4 】 否

My sister lives at the corner of Adams and Third.

【例 5 】 是

【例 6 】 否

This hobby began soon after the world saw the first postage stamp issued in Great Britain in 1840.

【例 7 】 否

Last but not least, salt has many other uses such as melting ice on roads in snowy regions!

【例 8 】 否

While TV shows vary from station to station, on the whole, early morning hours are dominated by news programs and evening hours by variety shows.

【例 9 】 否

They are concerned about how scientific the treatment is

【例 10 】 否

Emotional and physical hunger are both signals of emptiness, which you try to eliminate with food.

解答

作文範例：參考解答（P. 54）

【例 1 】 *For example / at the same time*

【例 2 】 *On the contrary / for example / Therefore*

【例 3 】 *Of course / However / Another / However / Finally*

【例 4 】 *First of all / therefore / Second / Last*

【例 5 】 *First of all / In other words / To sum up*

作文範例：參考解答（P. 59）

【例 1】

KTV is very popular in Taiwan, especially with city residents. Under the pressure of city life, many people love to sing in a KTV because they can relax and release their tension. With the low lighting and loud music, people easily forget their shyness and frustrations.

【例 2】

The house was beautiful. A long sidewalk led up to the door, and rows of flowers stood on either side of the steps. The front of the house was red brick with white woodwork.

【例 3】

My hometown is in the beautiful county of Ilan in northeastern Taiwan. Surrounded by mountains, Ilan has little traffic and has not been spoiled by swarms of visitors. Ilan is clean and quiet and claims to have the purest water on the island as its rivers are less polluted. It is a place of scenic beauty with green fields, mountains and rivers.

【例 4】

Of all the sports, swimming is my favorite. *Firstly*, it is beneficial to my health. It can make me stronger and more energetic and help to keep me slim. *Besides*, it's a good feeling to jump into the cool water on a hot summer day.

解答

【例5】

It is often said that health is wealth. This suggests that we should aim for health in the same way that many people aim for wealth. *In fact*, the goal of good health is much easier to achieve than that of wealth, since if we start trying to be healthy, the results are immediate and concrete. Money, *meanwhile*, can take a long time to accumulate.

歷屆考題觀摩：參考解答（P. 62）

【例1】 C / B / D / A / E

【例2】 D / E / A

【例3】 G / B / D / A

【例4】 B / A / E / D / H

【例5】 B / E / F / A / G / H

作文範例：參考解答（P. 71）

【例1】 *Indeed*, these methods really helped the Romans organize their empire well.

【例2】 *In short*, the school day at the University of Paris was a long and hard one.

【例3】 *Consequently*, the South became one of the nation's most progressive areas.

【例4】 *For all these reasons*, I believe that technology is of great benefit to today's students.

解
答

【例 5】 *In short*, it is important that we do not give up when working for our goals.

【例 6】 *To sum up*, I prefer to travel with a companion rather than travel alone.

【例 7】 *In sum*, taking our time when we do things has several advantages.

【例 8】 *In short*, this kind of friend is the best of all possible friends because he is my friend through both good times and bad.

【例 9】 *In short*, self-employment offers more freedom than either owning a business or working for someone else.

【例 10】 *For all of the above reasons*, I believe that we should preserve our historic buildings.

作文範例：參考解答（P. 84）

【例 1】 Most students feel that the uniforms are uncomfortable and unnecessary.

【例 2】 But it is rather easy if you keep the following suggestions in mind.

【例 3】 Discovering ways to improve their English is a problem which baffles many students.

作文範例：參考解答（P. 90）

【例1】 ***In short***, nowadays it is very important to maintain a habit of reading if we are to be successful in the world.

【例2】 ***In sum***, to learn from failure is an important key to success no matter who we are or what we do.

【例3】 ***In conclusion***, watching movies at home is generally cheaper and more comfortable than going to a theater.

【例4】 ***In a word***, without oil the world would stop moving.

【例5】 ***To sum up***, life is a series of experiences.

歷屆考題觀摩：參考解答（P. 93）

【例1】 C / A / D / E / B

【例2】 B / C / A / D

【例3】 E / A / D / B / C / F

【例4】 D / E / C / B / A

【例5】 E / B / C / A / D / F

解

答

英文作文轉承語背誦比賽

1. 口試辦法： 只要將本書p.1的英文轉承語背至2分鐘內，正確無誤，就算通過。

1.
- **First** 首先
  = Firstly
  = First of all
- = In the first place
  = To begin with
  = To start with
- = For starters
  = For openers
  = For one thing

- **At first** 最初
  = Initially
  = Originally
  = At the outset
- = At the beginning
  = From the beginning
  = From the start

2.
- **Second** 第二
  = In the second place
  Third 第三
  = In the third place
- **Then** 然後
  = **Next** 其次
- = Afterward(s) 之後
  = After this
  = Thereafter

- = Later
  = Later on
- = After a while
  = Following that
- = By and by
  = Subsequently
- **Soon** 很快
  = Shortly
  = Presently

2. 獎勵辦法： 優先背好的前100名讀者，可得「鍋寶超真空保溫杯」一個。背英文轉承語，不僅可以快速組織英文作文結構，講話都變得有邏輯，有條不紊，思考變清晰，一舉兩得。

3. 口試時間： 每日下午3點至晚上10點

4. 口試地點： 台北市許昌街17號6F
（捷運M8出口·壽德大樓）

✎ 得獎感言：

....

....

....

....

....

....

....

「鍋寶超真空保溫杯」領獎表

姓 名		手 機	
地 址			
教育程度：□小學　　□國中　　□高中　　□大學　　□研究所			
是否為劉毅英文班內生？　□是　　□否			

LE 劉毅英文教育機構　台北本部：台北市許昌街17號6F　　TEL：(02) 2389-5212
台中總部：台中市三民路三段125號7F　TEL：(04) 2221-8861
www.learnschool.com.tw

如何寫英文作文

主　　　編 / 劉　毅

發　行　所 / 學習出版有限公司　　　☎ (02) 2704-5525

郵　撥　帳　號 / 05127272 學習出版社帳戶

登　記　證 / 局版台業 2179 號

印　刷　所 / 文聯彩色印刷有限公司

台　北　門　市 / 台北市許昌街 10 號 2 F　　　☎ (02) 2331-4060

台灣總經銷 / 紅螞蟻圖書有限公司　　　☎ (02) 2795-3656

本公司網址　www.learnbook.com.tw

電　子　郵　件　learnbook@learnbook.com.tw

售價：新台幣二百五十元正

2017 年 6 月 1 日初版

高三同學要如何準備「升大學考試」

　　考前該如何準備「學測」呢？「劉毅英文」的同學很簡單，只要熟讀每次的模考試題就行了。每一份試題都在7000字範圍內，就不必再背7000字了，從後面往前複習，越後面越重要，一定要把最後10份試題唸得滾瓜爛熟。根據以往的經驗，詞彙題絕對不會超出7000字範圍。每年題型變化不大，只要針對下面幾個大題準備即可。

準備「詞彙題」最佳資料：

背了再背，背到滾瓜爛熟，讓背單字變成樂趣。

　　考前不斷地做模擬試題就對了！

你做的題目愈多，分數就愈高。不要忘記，每次參加模考前，都要背單字、背自己所喜歡的作文。考壞不難過，勇往直前，必可得高分！

練習「模擬試題」，可參考「學習出版公司」最新出版的「7000字學測英文模擬試題詳解」。我們試題的特色是：

①以「高中常用7000字」為範圍。②經過外籍專家多次校對，不會學錯。③每份試題都有詳細解答，對錯答案均有明確交待。

「克漏字」如何答題

　　第二大題綜合測驗（即「克漏字」），不是考句意，就是考簡單的文法。當四個選項都不相同時，就是考句意，就沒有文法的問題；當四個選項單字相同、字群排列不同時，就是考文法，此時就要注意到文法的分析，大多是考連接詞、分詞構句、時態等。克漏字是考生最弱的一環，你難，別人也難，只要考前利用這種答題技巧，勤加練習，就容易勝過別人。

準備「綜合測驗」（克漏字）可參考「學習出版公司」最新出版的「7000字克漏字詳解」。

本書特色：

1. 取材自大規模考試，英雄所見略同。
2. 不超出7000字範圍，不會做白工。
3. 每個句子都有文法分析。一目了然。
4. 對錯答案都有明確交待，列出生字，不用查字典。
5. 經過「劉毅英文」同學實際考過，效果極佳。

「文意選填」答題技巧

　　在做「文意選填」的時候，一定要冷靜。你要記住，一個空格一個答案，如果你不知道該選哪個才好，不妨先把詞性正確的選項挑出來，如介詞後面一定是名詞，選項裡面只有兩個名詞，再用刪去法，把不可能的選項刪掉。也要特別注意時間的掌控，已經用過的選項就劃掉，以免重複考慮，浪費時間。

準備「文意選填」，可參考「學習出版公司」最新出版的「7000字文意選填詳解」。

特色與「7000字克漏字詳解」相同，不超出7000字的範圍，有詳細解答。

「閱讀測驗」的答題祕訣

① 尋找關鍵字——整篇文章中，最重要就是第一句和最後一句，第一句稱為主題句，最後一句稱為結尾句。每段的第一句和最後一句，第二重要，是該段落的主題句和結尾句。從「主題句」和「結尾句」中，找出相同的關鍵字，就是文章的重點。因為美國人從小被訓練，寫作文要注重主題句，他們給學生一個題目後，要求主題句和結尾句都必須有關鍵字。

② 先看題目、劃線、找出答案、標號——考試的時候，先把閱讀測驗題目瀏覽一遍，在文章中掃瞄和題幹中相同的關鍵字，把和題目相關的句子，用線畫起來，便可一目了然。通常一句話只會考一題，你畫了線以後，再標上題號，接下來，你找其他題目的答案，就會更快了。

③ 碰到難的單字不要害怕，往往在文章的其他地方，會出現同義字，因為寫文章的人不喜歡重覆，所以才會有難的單字。

④ 如果閱測內容已經知道，像時事等，你就可以直接做答了。

準備「閱讀測驗」，可參考「學習出版公司」最新出版的「7000字閱讀測驗詳解」，本書不超出7000字範圍，每個句子都有文法分析，對錯答案都有明確交待，單字註明級數，不需要再查字典。

「中翻英」如何準備

可參考劉毅老師的「英文翻譯句型講座實況DVD」，以及「文法句型180」和「翻譯句型800」。考前不停地練習中翻英，翻完之後，要給外籍老師改。翻譯題做得越多，越熟練。

「英文作文」怎樣寫才能得高分？

① 字體要寫整齊，最好是印刷體，工工整整，不要塗改。

② 文章不可離題，尤其是每段的第一句和最後一句，最好要有題目所說的關鍵字。

③ 不要全部用簡單句，句子最好要有各種變化，單句、複句、合句、形容詞片語、分詞構句等，混合使用。

④ 不要忘記多使用轉承語，像 *at present*（現在），*generally speaking*（一般說來），*in other words*（換句話說），*in particular*（特別地），*all in all*（總而言之）等。

⑤ 拿到考題，最好先寫作文，很多同學考試時，作文來不及寫，吃虧很大。但是，如果看到作文題目不會寫，就先寫測驗題，這個時候，可將題目中作文可使用的單字、成語圈起來，寫作文時就有東西寫了。但千萬記住，絕對不可以抄考卷中的句子，一旦被發現，就會以零分計算。

⑥ 試卷有規定標題，就要寫標題。記住，每段一開始，要內縮5或7個字母。

⑦ 可多引用諺語或名言，並注意標點符號的使用。文章中有各種標點符號，會使文章變得更美。

⑧ 整體的美觀也很重要，段落的最後一行字數不能太少，也不能太多。段落的字數要平均分配，不能第一段只有一、兩句，第二段一大堆。第一段可以比第二段少一點。

準備「英文作文」，可參考「學習出版公司」出版的：